THE HIDDEN SPARK

Hope Colbère

CHIVERS
THORNDIKE

This Large Print book is published by BBC Audiobooks Ltd, Bath, England and by Thorndike Press®, Waterville, Maine, USA.

Published in 2005 in the U.K. by arrangement with Robert Hale Ltd.

Published in 2005 in the U.S. by arrangement with Robert Hale Ltd.

U.K. Hardcover ISBN 1–4056–3196–1 (Chivers Large Print)
U.K. Softcover ISBN 1–4056–3197–X (Camden Large Print)
U.S. Softcover ISBN 0–7862–7211–2 (General)

The text of this Large Print edition is unabridged.
Other aspects of the book may vary from the original edition.

Set in 16 pt. New Times Roman.

Printed in Great Britain on acid-free paper.

British Library Cataloguing in Publication Data available

Library of Congress Cataloging-in-Publication Data

Colbère, Hope.
      The hidden spark / by Hope Colbère.
         p.   cm.
      ISBN 0–7862–7211–2 (lg. print : sc : alk. paper)
      1. Highlands (Scotland)—Fiction. 2. Large type books. I. Title.

PR6053.O385H53 2005
823'.92—dc22   2004061680

Chapter One

The ambulance sent its strident warning ahead as it made the best possible pace it could through London's crowded streets. Coming from the direction of Royal Hospital Road, it sped along Lower Sloane Street, into Sloane Square; left into Draycott Place and thence to one of those quiet exclusive little squares off Draycott Avenue.

It drew up outside one of the flat fronted Regency houses, whose wide, cream enamelled front door stood open. A young policeman stood guard here, looking a little stunned and somewhat self-conscious; he had had to warn the small crowd, to '*Keep Back There*—per-lease! This way; stairs to your right.' This last to the two lean and wiry ambulance men who had approached the open door with urgent speed.

'Wot 'appened, mate?' one of them asked curiously as they manoeuvred the closed stretcher through the door, leaving a large indentation in the immaculate paintwork of the frame as they did so.

'An accidental shooting,' the young p.c. lied smoothly, and returned to his post to await the other expected ambulance, needed for the second but unmentioned casualty.

It was over fifteen minutes later before the

bearers returned, handling their grim load cautiously; their hardened nerves badly shaken at the sight they had found awaiting them. Without a word they took out the pitiful burden, ignoring the audible and somewhat cold-blooded comment from at least some of the spectators. Others, a little more feeling, gave only a quick glance at the covered form and looked hastily away. *All* wondered what had happened; *none* surmised correctly.

For Charles Helmann, financier and broker, had taken his own life—and his pitiful act was to almost destroy his only child.

A great many people were to shake their heads in stunned disbelief when it was blazened across the front pages of the morning papers, because this had been a tough, astute, and apparently well-satisfied man with surely *everything* to live for?

What only one or two actually knew, was that for some time Charles Helmann had been pretty close to bankruptcy; a fact which had not bothered him unduly until only six weeks before this horrific event. Hadn't he cut things finely before at least twice in his struggle for wealth? And each time hadn't he fought back, often ruthlessly, to become a little more wealthy than before?

Given time, he would have done so again; but—according to Miles Tremayne, Harley Street specialist, he had only three short months to live—maybe . . .

'I won't string you along Charles. It *could* be sooner. Why the devil didn't you come to me months ago?' His nice eyes had met the older man's with grave regret and a veiled distress. This was a friend of many years.

'No time! Had no inkling it could be this bad! I suppose you are—?' Helmann's look pleaded.

'Oh yes!' Tremayne broke in tersely. 'I am truly sorry, old man. Give anything to be able to tell you differently. What will you tell Nova? Like me to handle it?' He knew well Helmann's touchy pride.

'Good Lord no!—er—thanks. I must get a few things sorted out, but I shall not tell her—yet. Haven't been much of a companion to her since Fiona died, but can't burden her with this, poor kid.'

A sudden flare of panic and fear had passed fleetingly over the hard face, and was quickly suppressed. Shortly after he had left. That had been six weeks ago, and Tremayne had not seen his friend and patient again until just over an hour ago.

A shocked phone call from Burnes, the major domo to the compact establishment off Draycott Avenue owned by Helmann, had brought him within twenty minutes.

Inured as he was to injury and blood, the sight of Helmann, lying awkwardly between his big desk and a tall bookcase; half his head blown away, by a shot from the powerful navy

3

revolver clenched in convulsed fingers, had almost unnerved him. There was nothing he could do except call the police; which he started to do, looking up with alert eyes as a terrible scream came from somewhere along the same upper hallway . . .

Burnes began to tremble. 'It's Miss Nova sir. She—' he gulped, 'she found the Master.'

'Oh my God! Here, take over and get the law out here at once.'

Nova Helmann was sitting on her own big double bed and staring into space with wide unseeing eyes; her hands were clenched tightly and sweat was beading her smooth brow. She was screaming in regular, pitiful shrieks.

Miles Tremayne could deal with this and did so promptly. The two stinging blows stopped the nerve-shattering screams and the girl fell limply forward to be caught and laid gently back against her pillows.

Ten minutes and one powerful injection later, she lay quietly, like one dead; unaware, mercifully, of all the horror still going on in her father's study just a few yards away.

It was over an hour later when Tremayne left. The law had taken over quietly and efficiently. It had been the local Inspector who had found the suicide note, and a long envelope addressed 'To my dear daughter'.

A still shaky Burnes had told of his boss's retirement to his study straight after lunch; and of his order not to be disturbed until four-thirty, when he would like a pot of tea sent up. Miss Nova, when told of her father's request, had laughingly told them to put two cups on the tray and had run up happily enough to join her father for afternoon tea.

'Miss Nova had been extra happy because,' he stated nervously '—after hardly noticing her for over eight years, since the Missus died, in fact, her father had begun to make a lot more fuss of her this last six or so weeks.

'Also, Miss Nova had just become engaged. Last weekend it was, to a Mr Steven Blanchard. Very wealthy family! The governor had been pleased.'

The quietly authoritative man allowed him to chat on; then after the pitiful remains had been removed, and the sick girl taken off to Miles Tremayne's own small private nursing home in Wimbledon, the kindly Inspector suggested they all take the tablets left for them and get an early night.

'I'll leave P.C. Welton on duty,' he added, 'to keep the sightseers on the move! They'll soon give it up,' and he'd proved right.

In the quiet of his own lounge, Miles Tremayne was recounting the tragedy to his niece, Sara Arden. She and her parents were staying with him for a month before returning to Kinlochleven, where James Arden had a small practice.

Sara also happened to be an old school-friend of Nova's and her horror was expressed

5

in her warm, brown eyes as she faced her uncle.

'I'm afraid,' Miles concluded, 'that Nova is in for a bad time. Thank goodness we can keep the press away from her for a time at least. She'll need a friend badly, Sara my pet; there won't be many of 'em when this hits the headlines tomorrow.'

In the event he was proved to be right. In a matter of days it became public knowledge that Charles Helmann had died heavily in debt.

For three days, his shocked daughter lay heavily sedated; unaware of life around her, and when on the fourth day, Miles Tremayne decided to leave off sedation, she still lay inert and stunned, making no effort to rouse herself.

Her father's solicitor was anxious to see and talk to her, but Miles shook a doubtful head.

'It would be very unwise just now, Mr Balfour. Please give it a few more days,' and Henry Balfour had hung up, shaking his head in pity.

It had been Sara to whom Nova first paid real attention. Miles had wisely decided to let his niece be her first visitor, although her fiancé had asked to see her once or twice.

Even Tremayne had been aware of the relief with which his refusal was accepted by Blanchard and had wondered at it—briefly! He was a very busy man, with little time for vague unease.

6

Nova's small room was filled with the scent of mid-summer roses when Sara entered quietly and sat down gently by the narrow bed.

'Darling girl! How are you? We've all been so anxious about you!' Sara's voice was warm, but comfortably normal and Nova, for the first time in eight days really looked at another person.

'Hello, Sara dear,' she whispered huskily. 'It is nice of you to worry about me—but—but there's no need! I—I feel better about—about it now.'

She made a pathetic attempt to change the subject, waving a small limp hand at the two vases of pink and gold garden roses. 'S-Steven sent those yesterday. Lovely, aren't they? I h-hope Mr Tremayne will let him visit me soon.'

Sara controlled the lump in her throat with an effort. Never had she seen such a lost look in anyone's eyes; the shock of her horrific discovery must have been dreadful.

'They are beautiful aren't they? I know that Uncle Miles intends letting Steven see you very soon! He has asked several times, but you were rather poorly, dear. It's lovely to see you looking better.' She made a silent plea to be forgiven the lie. Nova looked awful!

Her beautiful eyes were heavily shadowed; her face pale and hollow-cheeked. She looked fragile and forlorn.

'My parents want you to come back to

7

Scotland with us at the end of September, Nova,' she continued brightly. 'I do hope that you will consider it, dear. Be lovely to have you!'

'Scotland? I—I believe I had a letter from d-dear old Lossie yesterday. Must read it again properly. S-she lives in . . . in . . . oh dear,' a distressed frown puckered the white brow as memory failed her.

'Never mind, you'll know when you read it again,' Sara broke in hastily. 'She has always kept in touch hasn't she? She used to be nanny to some friends of my father's you know. The Glencurrans.'

'I d-don't think I've heard of them, but yes, she writes to me at least four times a year.'

A moment later Sara rose to leave, pressing a gentle kiss on her friend's pale face.

'Mustn't overdo your first visit, dear. May I come again on Thursday? Bye-bye till then.'

Nova turned her face to the window and sighed. She knew there were many things she would have to face—and soon—but not just yet. When Steven came, he would support her with his love and protection. Their affection for each other was not of the spectacular kind, but he would be staunch in trouble—she was sure!

She slept without a sedative that night, but awoke early, after a grim nightmare of soft thuds behind a closed door; which she feared to open though a deep, male voice kept ordering her to do so . . .

Tremayne left orders to give her a mild sedation again. 'It won't be for long,' he comforted. 'You're getting along very well.'

But it was nearly a month before Nova was able to leave the little private sanitorium . . .

Chapter Two

'It isn't very good news I have to bring you, Miss Helmann,' Henry Balfour stated with regret, 'but out of the mess, your—er—ahem—father managed to tie up one or two things in your name, and *they* cannot be touched!' He cleared his throat again and anxiously eyed the listless figure seated by the window.

'Tell me about it please, Mr Balfour. *All* of it! I can't avoid trying to sort things out forever—can I?' A strained smile that did not reach the lovely eyes, sped briefly across her face.

'Well! I expect Tremayne has told you of your father's fatal illness. It came at a very bad time for him; he over speculated and was heavily in debt. Another nine months or so and he would have made a good recovery! However,'—he paused again, but Nova made no sign and he continued, 'if the town house is sold, also the farmhouse property in Kent, these will—or should—bring in enough to settle most things. Your father left the old Kentish farmhouse in *your* name, and also about £1,850, all he could raise in ready cash, so—er—you should be all right for a time. What—ahem—will you do Miss Helmann?' he asked at last, goaded by her apathetic silence.

Nova turned her listless gaze full on him.

'Oh, I don't know yet Mr Balfour! Certainly sell everything you can for me, *including* the little farmhouse in Kent. It will all help make amends to the p-people my father was indebted to. I would like to keep the cash and my few personal belongings—w-would *that* be in order?' She tilted her head at him and he nodded hastily.

'Good! Then of course, after a few months—I—I shall probably be getting married, but for the immediate future,' she sighed heavily, and her hands locked tautly round her crossed knees, 'I believe I may have an old friend to stay with me, until she returns to Scotland. She is very sweetly staying to help me over—over . . .'

Her voice faltered as she visualised her return to the house she had left under sedation just over four weeks ago. Sara was to assist her pack the things she would take with her into a new small flat—yet to be found!

She signed several papers for Balfour and then he left, wishing her a full recovery with warm sincerity and genuine sympathy.

That evening the two young women were quietly escorted to a waiting taxi by the matron, and it set off across the city, back to Draycott Avenue.

The staff, so soon to be leaving, welcomed the young lady of the house with warmth and cheerful normality, only their compassionate eyes showing their concern. Everything was just the same; only her father's presence was missing. For the first three or four days Nova could not bring herself to enter his study.

On the fourth day a huge bouquet arrived from Steven, with a note saying he would be back by the weekend and was anxious to see her. He had been on a business trip for nearly two weeks, but during his two or three visits to the nursing home, Nova had sensed a tension in him, caused she thought by worry at her illness.

'I *must* try and cheer up when he comes on Saturday,' she told Sara, and Sara had casually agreed.

By Saturday midday, at the end of that first week in September, the two girls had packed a fair amount of linen; chosen enough small pieces to furnish a flat; packed some of the lovely china and silver that had been Fiona Helmann's; two packing cases of Nova's personal clothing; a few books and her small collection of jewellery.

They had also to look over three small flats in the Chelsea area, on Monday and Tuesday of the following week. Nova had a very small income, left her by her mother, added to the modest sum left by her father, so she would not job hunt until settled into a new place.

Sara left to spend the evening with her uncle, and after a pleasant dinner she settled opposite him in front of the library fire to bring him up to date on Nova's progress.

'Between us, we've packed several things that she will keep, and Nova has arranged for a small amount of her mother's furniture to be stored, ready for the flat when found. She is quite adamant about the Kentish farmhouse too—but I don't know, Uncle Miles! Somehow, she still seems 'locked in' in spite of our busy efforts together!' Sara looked at her uncle's thoughtful face anxiously.

'Yes! You are quite right, my pet. Nova *is* still in a dangerous state. I'm hoping that the tension will go as she gets busier. The best way to return to normal is to *live* normally, and *if* nothing else occurs to set her back, Nova will soon be herself again—I hope!'

The object of their concerned discussion had been sitting in her own room waiting for her fiancé's ring at the front door. She had re-read the letter left her by her father, and felt again the surge of pity and love for a strong man beginning to feel the agony of the final stages of a fatal disease.

She *did* understand—she *did*! But oh! the great sense of loss after their new relationship. Why hadn't he shown affection for her always? Then again, the horror of her discovery flashed before her eyes, and she began to tremble.

Getting to her feet, Nova packed the letter into one of the two large suitcases nearby. The letter ended with her father's dearest love, and

13

regrets for the wasted years; she would keep it always, together with her darling Mimsey's few treasures. She turned to pick up her handbag and as she did so the doorbell rang. 'Must be Steven,' she thought and ran lightly down the white staircase.

Burnes was alone in the front hall . . . .

'It's a note for you, Miss Nova—delivered by hand.' His kind old face looked worriedly up at his young mistress, who held out a shaking hand numbly and turned to go back to her room.

Nova sat down before her dressing-table and read the note. It was from Steven, of course, and she read it through at least four times, then sat staring into space for several minutes.

Suddenly, she rummaged in her large leather handbag, until she found the letter she had received some weeks ago from Miss Agnes Lossiemuir, her old nanny. She read it through, then, with a strange, fixed look in her eyes, picked up the telephone . . .

Downstairs, Burnes and Mrs Prowse, the housekeeper, heard the faint pings as Nova used the extension phone in her room and relaxed with sighs of relief. Couldn't have been bad news; Miss Nova was obviously—they surmised—chatting to her fiancé on the phone. They did not hear the girl go quietly downstairs carrying two fairly heavy suitacases, nor her cautious opening of the front door . . .

14

Without once looking back, Nova made her way to the corner of the close. A few moments later a taxi pulled up, as arranged over the phone, and she was gone!

At ten o'clock, a frantic Burnes phoned Miles Tremayne's house, and he and Sara made a wild dash through the city streets only just keeping within the speed limits.

It was Sara who found the two notes; one in Blanchard's writing, the other addressed simply to 'Dear Sara'.

'I want you to read Steven's letter, then you will understand why I must get away. *Please* don't worry about me—I *think* I shall be all right—*in time!* I have gone to Lossie; she will help me. I *will* write to you, dear Sara, I promise—when I feel better. Please thank Mr Tremayne for me, and wish Burnes and the others all the best in their new lives. Above all—*please* don't worry. Yours, gratefully always, Nova.'

'Oh, God!' Sara groaned. 'What on earth has . . .?' She reached out and opened the other note, reading it in silence. Her face whitened with anger and soundlessly she handed it to Miles.

It stated quite simply that Steven Blanchard considered that under the present circumstances, he would be unable to continue with their engagement.

'We've been such good friends, that I know you will understand my family's position. It reflects in no way upon your own character, my dear,—(Sara almost heard the unctuous voice utter the hateful words)—but being so much in the public eye, my father must be so very careful. I hope that you will be a dear about this and allow our associates to think it was a mutual agreement?'

Even Tremayne had gasped at this. He looked up with eyes black with anger. 'I only hope,' he uttered forcefully, 'that this unspeakable person hasn't triggered off more than Nova can cope with!' He met Sara's horrified gaze calmly. 'Who is Lossie? And where does she live?' he asked urgently.

'S-she is Nova's ex-nurse, Uncle Miles, and stayed with her for over two years after Mrs Helmann died. Nova was over seventeen when she left, but—oh dear! I just don't know where she is now. Somewhere in Scotland—I *think*! Perhaps Burnes or Mrs Prowse or Milly may know?'

Burnes remembered her all right but apart from knowing that she'd been left a cottage in Scotland, by her old father, he didn't know whereabouts.

They searched for old letters or address books in vain. Nova had *really* cleared out unwanted articles; and the only notice of Miss Lossiemuir's address was travelling with her at this moment, on the ten-fifteen to Oban.

At eleven o'clock, a weary Sara remembered the Glencurrans and phoned

Glencurran Castle, only a few miles from her parents' home in Kinlochleven. A sleepy housekeeper answered her call with obvious surprise and informed her regretfully that Mistair Ross was away on his wee bit island and wouldna' be back for six or s'en weeks, ye ken! Could ye no' reet to him? So a despondent Sara took Ross Glencurran's island address, which turned out to be miles away in Invernesshire, and sat down to write an urgent letter at once.

Miles offered to post it on his way home as she saw him out.

'Funny how I've never seen Ross's island in all these years,' she told herself aloud. They had known the family for some six years now. 'I'll wait a few days to see if he can help me trace Lossie, or to see if Nova writes, then I'll return to Kinlochleven. I only hope that Steven Blanchard doesn't cross my path! I shall forget I'm a lady!' And with an unhappy sigh she prepared for bed.

Chapter Three

As one in a dream, Nova had entered the train at St Pancras after booking right through to Oban. She had registered the fact that she would change at Glasgow, but scarcely took in the booking clerk's puzzled look at her pale, almost blank face. She only knew that all her facial muscles felt stiff and sore, as though she had wept for hours.

Some strange instinct bid her act as normally as possible, so she accepted a hot drink and retired to her sleeping berth; there to sleep heavily, but without real rest.

Arrived in Glasgow at a very early hour, a kindly porter put the heavy cases on the train for Oban; accepting the tip given with a blank and unreal smile, with a worried frown on his grubby, open face. 'Yon lassie looks ill!' he muttered to himself, but as she settled back in her seat without another glance in his direction, he went off shaking his head.

The train left soon after, and Nova roused herself long enough to take out and re-read Lossie's letter. The address was Rowan Cottage, Ardslignish, Inverness. Lossie expressed her tender sympathy, coupled with sound Scots sense, and begged that she (Nova), would come and stay a wee while to get over things. 'You can get over to me from

Oban,' she stated, 'but let me know if and when you decide to come and I'll send you full instructions.' A bleak little smile touched Nova's mouth briefly. All she had done was to send a telegram last night. Lossie would be ready to make her welcome, she was sure, and at the thought of seeing that sturdy, fifty-eight year old figure; with the greying, sandy-coloured hair and twinkling eyes, Nova felt an inexpressible longing to be held and mothered.

She fought down the threatening tears with an effort and closed her eyes; seeing nothing of the early morning beauty of the Highlands as the train sped on—on—through Stirling, Callander, Lochearnhead, Crianlarich, Dalmally and finally Oban.

Here she left the train, almost dragging her heavy cases, and stood forlornly looking around her until another kindly station official approached.

'Can I help ye, Missie? Ye look a mite lost!'

Nova smiled vaguely, and then pulled herself together with an effort. 'Oh! thank you. I-I am a bit! C-could you please suggest a quiet hotel and perhaps—a taxi?'

'Weel—er—try the Lancaster. It's verra good! I'll get ye a cabbie.' He stepped out and signalled to a taxi just cruising up to the station entrance and in a few moments Nova was on her way.

She booked in at the pleasant hotel for one night only, and spent that strangely unreal day making enquiries on how to reach Ardslignish. It involved a longish steamer trip, so she listlessly booked for the following day, and returned to her hotel.

She ate a modest tea, some inner voice warning her that missing out on so many meals—she'd had no lunch—would not help her reach Lossie on whose comfortable bosom she ached to lay her weary, and stunned head.

The kindly staff, still fairly busy at the beginning of this second week in September, nevertheless found time to discuss their latest guest, wondering at her paleness. One surmised that she was recovering from a severe illness; another was troubled by a faint recollection of having seen her before somewhere . . .

Nova, still suffering from the horrors of morbid curiosity, and always dreading recognition since her picture had been on the front pages of most national papers, would have trembled with fear had she known of this. Apart from pulling back her hair into a chignon and wearing no make-up, she had been too sick at heart to attempt serious disguise. Luckily the severe style and the drawn paleness of her face changed her sufficiently from the smiling, glowing girl pictured for the likeness to be elusive.

After a very restless night, Nova awoke unrefreshed, and burning with eagerness to be gone. Trying hard to fill in the waiting hours, she went for a short stroll along the esplanade, still without seeing the overwhelming beauty of the scenery on all sides.

In the golden beauty of a midday in September, she sat in a sheltered corner of the steamer, alone, and unaware of the curious glances that were thrown her way.

Disembarking at Tobermory, Nova almost gave up in frustrated despair when informed that she would have to hire a private cabin cruiser to take her across to Ardslignish. Her distress showed so openly that a middle-aged woman who had glanced her way several times, stepped forward in concern.

'Why, my dear! I'm going over—to Glenbeg! It's a couple of miles on, but we can share the same hiring. Sam McNeil usually runs me over.' Her healthy, broad Scots face smiled kindly at the girl. 'Tell you what, come and have a cup of tea with me, then we'll go down to the jetty together. I've booked him for four o'clock.'

Nova's spiritual exhaustion, added to the weariness of body was so great by now, that she accepted the proffered help thankfully.

During tea, complete with toasted tea cakes and apple pie, Nova learned that the good samaritan's name was Laura Conway; that she and her husband Charles (Nova flinched at the name) ran the small Post Office cum store at Glenbeg and that she had been spending a week with her married son in Tobermory. 'And

21

now,' she concluded cheerfully, 'I'll be glad to get home again, tho' I love to visit Jamie! Charles and I go together for two weeks in May, then our son and his wife and two sons come to us on and off all summer and every other Christmas.'

Nova tried hard to take in the pleasantly normal conversation and to respond, but failed miserably.

'I'm s-so sorry,' she said helplessly, 'I've been rather ill—and the—the journey has been so tiring.' At Mrs Conway's questioning, sympathetic look, 'I'm on my way to spend a few weeks with my old nurse, Miss Lossiemuir. Do you know her?'

'Agnes Lossiemuir! Why yes! She's an old friend of mine! She lives only about two miles from us. We even deliver her groceries! But my dear, should you have travelled all this way alone—from London?—after an illness?'

Nova dropped her eyes quickly. 'I didn't realise—and—and I did prefer to be alone.'

Laura hesitated to pry further, but as the girl gave her a faint smile of gratitude, she also was teased by a faint recollection—of what? Even up here, in the heart of the Highlands, news had a far reaching impact, but again, it eluded the stirred chords of memory.

Sam McNeil, with Scots taciturnity, accepted Nova's inclusion on his sparse passenger list and about forty-five minutes later obligingly dropped her off at a tiny wooden jetty and pointed out Rowan Cottage, standing alone at the end of a wide gravel path some two hundred feet away. There were a few other grey stone cottages at intervals between the little beach and Rowan Cottage, and McNeil whistled shrilly at the sturdy lad, a boy of about twelve, playing with a small terrier outside the nearest one.

'Hey! Donal', will ye no' gi'e the leddy a han' wi' her bags?'

The boy ran up eagerly. 'I weel that,' he avowed cheerfully, and lifted both cases only to put the lighter one down again. 'I'll ha' to come back for thissen,' he said, and followed Nova towards Rowan Cottage.

She turned at the entrance to the lane and waved to the boat as it pulled away from the little jetty. Far out to the left as she gazed blankly, a cabin cruiser was preparing to leave a small green island, but she was not interested enough to watch it and turned back to follow the boy to the cottage.

He dumped the heavy case with a sigh of relief and set off back up the lane to get the other one.

With a sense of finding a haven at last, Nova stepped into the stone porch and rapped loudly on the shining brass knocker. It only dawned on her gradually, that the cottage was unusually quiet. Surely there would have been some movement from within? Why hadn't Lossie opened the door to her loud knocking?

By the time Donald returned with her other case, the sick, stunned look was back in the beautiful, tragic eyes . . .

He hurried up, panting beneath his load.

'Me mam says that Miss Lossiemuir was called awa' two days sin'; to 'er sister over at Strontian. Seems she was taken queer.' He paused for breath, wondering at the stricken look, beyond his understanding, on the young 'leddy's' face.

'It's all right, Donald,' Nova heard an unreal voice (was it her own?) say. 'I half expected her to be gone by now—tell your mother not to worry, Miss Lossiemuir left the—the back door key—with—with—' her mind searched frantically, 'Mrs Conway. I can let myself in.' With this lie, she handed the satisfied boy a tenpenny piece and watched him skip off.

She gave a shuddering sigh and turned to stare hopelessly at the solid closed door. The idea that maybe she could get in somehow through a window, or the back way, entered her head, and she almost ran round to the back. Here, also, all was solidly locked, and the sanctuary she so badly needed barred to her.

Nova sank on to the wooden bench in the small back porch and closed her eyes . . .

She stayed this way for some time, then a little chilly wind invaded her tiny shelter and she held her gold wrist watch close to her eyes, peering in the pearly, fading light. It said ten to seven. Had she sat here for so long? Almost two hours!

It came to her suddenly what she must do! By crossing at a sharp angle from the top of the little lane, Nova avoided the few cottages and made her way, as one in a trance, to the end of the tiny jetty thrusting out some thirty feet into the darkening, ruffled waters of Loch Sunart.

Donald and his parents had set off over ten minutes before to walk the two miles to Glenbeg, untroubled, as both had accepted the stranger's story. She knew Laura Conway didn't she? They themselves had seen them waving to each other earlier on as the ferry boat left.

The cabin cruiser that Nova had seen almost subconsciously on her arrival, as it was leaving the little island some five hundred yards out into the loch, began its return trip. It was the only moving thing on the loch, and as Nova was facing away from it as it left Glenbeg and ran towards the island, she didn't see it.

The man at the wheel saw the figure of a girl, a knee length coat blowing back from her body, shoulder length dark hair lifting in the lively breeze, and slowed his motor to watch.

His dark brows drew together and he took his pipe from between strong teeth, stabbing it towards the silhouetted figure and addressing the sturdy man leaning behind him in the cabin's interior.

'Jock! Here, quick! Take over will you? I've

got a feeling . . .' He swung the boat back towards the jetty as he spoke and his companion, used to instant action, took his place.

He was half out of his heavy, knitted jersey when the splash came to them.

'I damn well knew it!' he muttered, and dived away from the boat which Jock promptly ran up to the jetty.

Here he tied alongside and hurried into the saloon, where he switched on the lights, spread a canvas over the long upholstered settee and from the aft cabin took a thick, gaily-coloured blanket.

He then returned to the wheel-house to await results, peering through the rapidly fading light in time to see his boss wading on to the shallow beach with a limp form held high against him. Moments later he took the girl from Ross Glencurran's arms and laid her on the prepared settee, wrapping her closely in the blanket.

It took Ross five minutes to strip off in the tiny shower-room and get into dry spares, then still rubbing his wet hair, he entered the saloon and sat down to gaze thoughtfully at the small, pallid face lying beside him. Jock came and stood at his elbow.

'Is it help she'll be needing to get breathin' agin' boss?' he asked anxiously.

'No fear Jock! I practically followed her in. She hadn't time to swallow too much! But what bothers me is I think she deliberately jumped in and seemed very much to resent being—er—rescued! I'm afraid she's out like this—' his cool, hazel eyes met the other man's, 'because I hit her!'

Chapter Four

They say a drowning person sees the whole of his life flash by but Nova had spent the two lonely hours in Lossie's back porch reviewing her short life up to the moment of her unhappy decision to hide away from life and its cruelties . . .

Indulged and over-protected by her beloved Mimsey, (her own pet name for her mother) who had spent all of her daughter's growing up period trying to make her husband show more open affection for their little daughter, Nova had always felt a deep sense of rejection. Whilst dutifully giving his little girl all the worldly necessities and quite a few luxuries, Charles Helmann had not hidden his disappointment that their only child was a girl.

Because her mother felt his passive rejection of the little girl, the child felt it too, and it was only Nova's nanny who saved them both from becoming morbid about it.

'Och! dinna fash yersels' aboot it,' she advised. 'Like enough, he'd miss ye if ye weren't aboot.'

Just after Nova's twelfth birthday Mimsey became ill, and after a battle lasting nearly three years, the surgeons had to admit defeat. She died a few days after Nova's fifteenth birthday.

After a few precious weeks of shared grief, her father turned again to the financial world he lived for, and became even more deeply involved in his efforts to assuage his loss.

By her eighteenth birthday Lossie had gone back to Scotland, to nurse her old father through his last two years of life. Nova had taken a part time job, helping a friend of her mother's run a fine antique shop in Chelsea.

She had met Steven Blanchard at one of her father's small business dinners about four years ago. At nineteen, she had at first found him too smooth and sleek, but his manners were always so charming and he had a quiet self-confidence so that gradually the young Nova, vaguely flattered by his sophisticated attention, had formed an affectionate, sexless attachment for him which it suited him well to encourage.

Their engagement just after Nova's twenty-third birthday had surprised no one, and this, coupled with her father's closer companionship had seemed to make her feel needed as never before.

During the first weeks of her illness Nova had scarcely noted how many of her father's so-called friends had quietly dropped away. Sara Arden had remained staunch; also Miles Tremayne and her father's solicitor friend. She had had flowers from her employer and the letter of sympathy from Lossie. The flowers from Steven she had taken for granted, as she had his loyalty . . .

Until she had received the cowardly note from Steven breaking their engagement, the only aspect of her father's death to shock her had been the terrible sight that had met her horrified eyes. The shock had been purely and terribly physical. Blanchard's note had brought her shame and despair at a time when she was totally unfitted for either.

Lossie's absence had been the final straw, and Ross Glencurran had been quick to notice the implications as he had watched the girl throw a last despairing look at the beach and clasp her hands to her head as she seemed to sway before falling.

Watching the pale face, with its long, dark lashes lying wetly against the smooth skin, his mouth tightened grimly as he recalled the gasping cry of 'Don't don't! Let me go down— please,' and the way she had thrown up her arms in surrender to the grey waters of Loch Sunart.

He leaned forward to dry her face with his towel, then shifting his position, lifted her across his lap and pulled off the heavy, wet coat. By the time Jock came back from the galley with hot coffee laced with brandy, the girl was down to a thin silk slip, from which Ross had managed to press out most of the water with the towel.

He lifted her while the dour Jock placed a dry blanket under her, and then holding her firmly in one arm, he wrapped her warmly again.

As he folded it tightly around her shoulders, he felt the slight form shudder, and found himself gazing into the loveliest, almost violet-blue eyes he had ever seen . . .

Their expression, blank at first, slowly deepened to the most despairing look.

'My sainted aunt,' he thought. 'Whatever could have caused such a look as that?' Aloud, he said sternly, 'Good! You've saved me the need of slapping you awake! Here, drink this.' And holding her head pressed against him, Glencurran placed the beaker of hot coffee firmly against the pallid lips.

Nova obediently drained the beaker and felt the warmth permeate her chilled limbs but she felt nothing but reproach for the man who had dragged her from the icy loch. She closed her eyes against the closeness of his scrutiny and very quietly went to sleep.

'Well I'll be—' Glencurran turned to his amazed companion. 'Head for Curransay, Jock. Meg will make the lassie comfortable for tonight at least.' He laid the sleeping girl down gently before adding, 'There's something familiar about her—but I can't place it. I'll pop back to the Conways later on, see if they know anything about her. I'm sure I saw her getting off Sam McNeil's boat earlier on.'

'Ay! ye did! I saw her mesen' as we crossed. Young Donal' was taking her along towards

Rowan, ye ken.'

'Must be a young friend of Lossie's then. We'll find out soon enough, I guess.'

Just over half an hour later, Jock's wife had the still sleeping girl dry and warm, and tucked up with hot water bottles.

She hadn't even roused from the deep sleep that was half shock, half complete fatigue when Jock had handed her up to Glencurran's arms and he had carried her to the house, and thence up the stairs. Here, the sturdy Meg, in no whit ruffled, had taken over.

'What treasures you two are!' Ross smiled at her.

'Och! awa wi ye, laddie, and get ye dinner. Ye'll serve yersel', but 'tis all ready. Now off ye go!'

But Glencurran called out to Jock that he was off back to Glenbeg.

Twenty minutes later, he startled the Conways by thumping vigorously on their back door.

'Why Mr Ross dear, what's up?' Laura asked as Charles showed their visitor into the cosy living-room behind the store.

'It's all right Mrs Conway! I just want to know if you can tell me anything about the young lady who got off at Ardslignish earlier today?' He smiled pleasantly but the hazel eyes were keen.

'Why yes—a little. It seems she came from London to spend a few weeks with Agnes

Lossiemuir, who was once her nurse. Poor child was recovering from an illness and really looked exhausted. Nothing has happened to her, has it?' she added sharply.

'Why Laura! I forgot you didn't know! Miss Lossiemuir was called to her sister's in Strontian two days ago,' Charles Conway broke in. 'A telegram came for her quite late on Saturday and I phoned it to her at her sister's house. She was rather upset about it! It seems her widowed sister had broken a leg, and Miss Lossiemuir will not be home for at least three weeks.' He had turned to Glencurran with this explanation, adding with a glance that included his wife's kindly, concerned face, 'As a matter of fact, dear, she asked if we could keep the young lady with us until she returns! I—er—I forgot about it until now,' he admitted unhappily.

'Oh dear! Has the girlie found shelter at one of the Ardslignish cottages, do you know, Mr Ross?' she queried anxiously.

'No! I believe she was on her way to the Kerrs' place though, when Jock and I saw her—er—faint. We landed and gathered her in. She's quite safe over with Meg Graham. The girl *was* pretty tired,' a small, tight smile twisted the strong mouth. 'But don't worry yourselves, she will be well looked after until Lossie gets back. I'll come over in the morning and give her a ring.' He smiled evenly at them both, then turned to go.

'Oh! by the way,' he stopped just inside the door, 'as she went to sleep almost at once, I hadn't time to ask. What is her name? D'you know?'

'The telegram simply said "Nova",' Charles stated.

'And did you find her cases?' Laura broke in. 'Young Donald took them down to Rowan for her.'

'I'll go along now and pick 'em up,' Ross assured her easily. 'Goodnight and thank you both.'

He kept his own powerful car garaged in an outhouse at the back of the Conways' house, and it took only minutes to cover the two miles to Ardslignish. Here he found not only two very heavy cases, but the girl's handbag, with her initials in gold, 'N.H.'.

Again a faint memory teased him. 'Nova,' he said aloud as he sped back to Glenbeg, 'Nova—little new star. Why *does* the name seem vaguely familiar!'

It was gone nine when he got back to Curransay Island, where he promptly informed an interested couple of his discoveries concerning their guest.

'Poor wee lassie,' Meg uttered. 'Oh weel! She'll be safe here for a bit. I'll like to build her up and get some roses in those pale cheeks.'

The two men exchanged quick glances, one wondering if it would be wise to tell her of the

34

girl's possible attempt on her own life, the other with every intention of putting her very fully in the picture as he would need her cooperation and understanding, if they were to help the girl over the next week or so.

But Meg Graham had already come to her own conclusions. Fell in the loch indeed! Did her good man and the boss take her for a fool? But for once she was wrong. Nova *had* slipped and had merely ceased to fight—hence her resentment at being saved . . . !

Chapter Five

Ross, who rarely rushed anywhere, strolled down to his own little stone jetty just after eight-thirty on Tuesday morning. He had given Meg and Jock the job of keeping a very close eye on their guest who was still sleeping soundly, but he had no intention of taking chances with her probable actions, should she wake up and find herself quite unattended.

Over an early breakfast he and Meg had talked about it.

'I'll know a bit more when I come back,' he stated firmly. 'Lossie is sure to have a story of some sort to tell me. I'll play it by ear from there, and we can stick together with the same explanations, eh!'

So Jock had taken a chair outside the slightly open door, and had promised to yell for Meg at the very first sound from within.

'Don't rush in yersel', forbye,' she warned him, 'the lassie has nowt on but her skin and belike ye'll scare her witless!'

The two men had exchanged brief grins, and now Ross was on his way over to Glenbeg, to use the only public call box within thirty miles.

He could see the Conways preparing to open the shop through the windows, and waved a casual hand before starting his call. This was to Miss Lossiemuir to whom he explained briefly, but succinctly, the circumstances of his meeting with her young friend.

'Och no! Poor bairn! I canna think what iver possessed her to do such a thing! I thought that she was getting weel again! I expect ye know of the tragedy—ye dinna? Weel . . .' and she told him of the girl's terrible experience.

'So *that's* who she is! Why Lossie, yes, I do recall the affair—about seven weeks ago, wasn't it? Still—ghastly as it was for her, d'you really think it was sufficient in itself to have caused the child to do such a thing?' He sounded puzzled and not a little stern.

'Och! I dinna ken, my dear! She has been verra ill; perhaps she got frightened because I wasna' at hame! Och! I wisht I'd been there!'

'Now, now, Lossie! Not to worry. She's safe enough with Meg Graham. Just give me the London address or phone number and I'll simply tell them that she is safe with you at Rowan. No good letting *everyone* know what happened, so keep it quiet, eh? After all, it *may* have been an accident.'

They spoke for a few seconds longer then, promising to keep in touch, he rang off.

Charles Conway looked up as Glencurran entered the little shop and asked coolly how they were off for change.

'I want to phone London and won't take too kindly to being cut off every three minutes,' Ross informed the kindly postmaster.

37

'Surely, Mr Glencurran,' Conway smiled pleasantly. 'Why don't you use the private line and ask the exchange for a charge? You'd be very welcome!' He had been carefully sorting the overnight mail as he spoke and suddenly gave an exclamation. 'Here's a London marked letter for you, sir,' and he handed over a thick, pale blue envelope, before turning discreetly to his task.

Ross took the letter to the door and read it through thoroughly, in his unhurried, deliberate way. Then he read it through again, but the cold glitter of his hazel eyes boded ill for someone; the strong mouth had a cruel twist that would have caused the unaware Nova to tremble, so menacing was it.

'I'll take you up on that kind offer, Mr Conway,' his voice came suddenly to the older man.

'I'll just warn Laura not to barge through while you are busy, Mr Glencurran.' And Ross sat down by the little phone table with a grateful nod.

'Sara my dear,' he murmured some moments later to the eager far off voice that answered his call. 'I have your letter . . . *and* your little friend!' He ignored the little cry of relief and continued. 'As luck would have it Lossie lives only two or three miles from Curransay. What your Uncle Miles feared, did I *think* happen! But the girl is OK for the time being. I've had a chat to Lossie, who is held up

38

in Strontian for about three weeks. I was puzzled as to the girl's reason for possibly doing such a thing, but your letter explains it only too clearly, poor kid! I'll ring Lossie again after this. Er—one question, was the girl so very much in love with that rat?'

In spite of her concern Sara almost laughed at this blunt query. 'I don't think she was, Ross. They sort of drifted into it in a convenient way. The real trouble was that Nova had been mentally depending on him to supply the help and support she was needing so badly after her illness. It was a cruel thing to do at such a time! Can I come and see her in a few days, Ross? I'm going back to Kinlochleven this weekend now that I know Nova is safe!'

Glencurran had his reservations about Nova's 'safety'. He had a feeling they were going to have a fight on their hands based purely on the wild despair he had glimpsed in the lovely violet eyes . . .

'Make it at least two weeks,' he said coolly. 'Give old Meg a chance to put some colour in her cheeks. She's very tired, and a bit off colour after her—er—dip in the loch!' He kept his voice deliberately casual in order to allay Sara's concern.

He said the same thing to Miss Lossiemuir a few moments later, after explaining the real cause of his young guest's distress so she tearfully agreed to stay put and write to

Miss Nova.

Half an hour later, after settling his phone bill and raiding the shop for chocolates, he thanked them again and left.

Turning to the right, he strolled along to a little stone cottage where a few moments chat induced old Angus MacKay to part up with a huge bunch of his golden chrysanthemums, and thus laden, a thoughtful Glencurran returned to his own domain.

'How's tricks?' he asked brightly, entering the big, clean kitchen to deposit his load.

'The lassie woke half an hour ago,' Jock told him. 'Meg has gone awa oop wi' her breakfast.' He silently eyed the glowing blossoms.

'Old Angus let me have 'em,' Ross exclaimed smoothly. 'They're better than ours! Help cheer her up! I want to talk to you and Meg in a few minutes, Jock. Any coffee going begging?'

The large beaker Jock filled for him was almost empty by the time Meg came back, wearing a very worried frown and shaking her head.

She set the still laden tray back on the big scrubbed table. 'The chil' has flatly refused t'touch a thing,' she stated helplessly.

His hazel eyes narrowed as he rose to his full height. 'Is that so,' he drawled, strolling towards the door. 'Well, don't worry Meggie. She'll be hungry enough tonight, so we'll just forget to take her lunch and tea, eh?' His white teeth flashed in a hard grin. 'I'll just pop up and have a quick chat—is she decent now?' And at Meg's speechless nod, 'Good! Stay handy,' and he took the stairs in threes.

Nova had been lying with closed eyes, her face towards the wall not seeing or caring anything about her surroundings. The first few hours of her deep sleep had been dreamless, but as the morning approached she had been tormented by terrible nightmares, first of her father, then of Blanchard, then of a terrible face that kept shouting at her from the depths of an icy lake until finally, all three dreams merged and she woke, sweating and trembling. The great tide of hopeless despair had swamped her again, so that she'd moaned with anguish.

Meg Graham, entering with a heavy tray, had been filled with pity as her kind eyes met the despairing, shadowed eyes turned towards her. 'Poor wee bairn,' she murmured. 'Ye'll ay feel better after I've freshed you up and ye've tuckit in to yer breakfast.'

The girl had merely groaned again and turned her face away but had submitted indifferently to a quick wash and to having a pretty nightdress slipped over her head. She had mutely refused the tray.

Glencurran stood a few feet away and gazed at the still figure lying in the big, old-fashioned bed. The curve of her cheek and chin were sweetly rounded, though ivory pale, and he

41

could see long, jet black, silken lashes by leaning slightly forward. Her hair had dried to glossy, blue-black, shoulder length curls, tangled and tumbled now.

'Miss Helmann, I know you are not asleep! Look at me, please.' The deep voice startled Nova into rolling over to turn a wide, violet-blue gaze on the speaker.

Ross encountered a look that almost stopped his heart, so filled was it with first, puzzlement, then recognition, followed by despair and deep reproach. A look that held intense dislike and certainly no gratitude.

'Oh yes!' he stated coldly. 'I can see you think I should have left you to drown, but let me tell you that having saved your life, I now consider it belongs to me, so I shall keep a strict eye on what you do with it in future! Do I make myself clear?' He leaned down and looked closely into the drawn face.

'I didn't ask you to save my life,' she whispered at last, 'and you can't watch me all the time. Fate may decide again—' She closed her eyes again.

Glencurran clenched his big fists to stop himself from shaking her into awareness. 'Somehow,' he thought desperately, 'I have to make her want to fight back.'

He carefully checked the room for any sharp or dangerous objects, even removing two big tasselled cords that held the curtains looped.

42

Later he went along to the bathroom and removed several articles.

'One of us will have to always stay around, until this melancholy goes,' he muttered.

Nova opened her eyes in time to see him leave, her tired mind busy planning and scheming, looking for another means of escape from the life she thought she had no further use for. 'It needn't be that way. I can just shut out the rest of the world. That way—nothing can hurt me again,' she told herself.

Chapter Six

By the end of the second day Meg and Jock were both beginning to feel the strain. Glencurran had told them of his findings and even the taciturn Jock had expressed pity. The three of them had taken it in turns to keep guard, but they need not have feared violence. Nova was already determined to shut out all humanity . . .

It was only as Meg prepared yet another tray—every other one had been steadily refused—that it occurred to Ross what the girl was trying to do; not starve to death exactly, but just to become too weakened to be forced to face up to living.

'Nearly three days without eating! Why the little—Here Meggie—*I'll* take this one up!' and exchanging a startled glance with her husband, Meg had stepped back to let him take the laden tray.

During their talk, Glencurran had told them of his intent to rouse the girl to a state of vigorous protest. 'She has this fixation about opting out of daily life because she feels there is nothing worthwhile left for her. I want to give her something to fight for. I want to *make* her hate *me* so much, it'll be more important to her than shutting herself off from everyone else!' He had paused with narrowed eyes.

'Whatever I do,' he added grimly, 'I want you to go along with it.' They had nodded staunch support but both had noticed his expression when he looked at their unwilling guest. It wasn't her hatred he really wanted!

The late September evening had turned chilly and Nova's room looked cheerful in soft lamplight, flickering flames from an open fire, and the golden flowers.

She lay staring at the ceiling, the hollow shadows on her small face bringing a pang of angry despair to the man who entered quietly to place the tray on the bedside table. His instinct was to reach out and crush her close, comforting and caressing, but he steeled himself as he reached out a brown hand to take her chin, forcing her head round to face him.

'So it's rudeness to those who would care for you now, is it?' he asked coldly. 'What makes you think I'll allow that, Miss Helmann?'

'I don't see what you can do about it,' Nova whispered weakly.

The grip on her chin tightened cruelly, so that she gave an involuntary cry of pain, putting up a small thin hand to push him away.

'Have you never heard of "force" feeding then? I don't think you're in a very fit state to fight about it, so unless you'd like me to demonstrate, I suggest you stop this nonsense and get on with your dinner.' His voice carried conviction, and for the first time, the blank eyes held a tiny flicker of fear.

Suddenly she made a helpless gesture. 'I—I don't think I could . . .! please . . .! You—you don't understand! Just go away and leave me alone.'

Her voice shook and she closed her eyes, only to open them wide again as she felt his arms go around her. He lifted her against him and piled the pillows behind her. Then he tucked her firmly into the crook of his arm.

'Right, if that's how you want it—here goes,' and he pulled a bowl of hot, thick soup towards him and picked up a spoon.

Nova went limp in his powerful hold, tipping up her head to his face. Her eyes registered bitter protest.

'All right—y-you win this time,' she murmured listlessly.

'Good!' was all he answered and he began feeding her the soup.

Because Nova was young and basically healthy, she found the soup delicious. How badly she had needed it! But when she protested, 'Enough, I can't honestly eat anymore,' half-way through an omelette, Ross, well satisfied, gave in.

'Meg will bring you up a hot, malted milk later on. Don't refuse it, will you?' There was no mistaking the threat in his voice.

Nova send him a peculiar look, half fear, half respect. 'No! I'm s-sorry to be such a nuisance to you all,' she whispered. 'How did you know my name?'

'I looked through your handbag. Yes,' answering the startled look, 'all your cases are here. I'll tell you more about it tomorrow. Goodnight, Miss Helmann. Be good!' And fully aware of the value of having even a small thing to wonder about, he left her.

Nova slept that night with the problem on her mind of how best could she quit this household without the intervention of the big man, whose name she did not even know! So wrapped up was she still in her own misery, that she didn't even *care* where she was. Nothing had really registered except the woman's name—Meg, and a faint dawning of fear and hatred of the domineering man!

Towards dawn the terrible dreams came again, so Nova awoke heavy-eyed, and very, very low in spirit. Meg, entering with her breakfast tray eyed her shadowed face nervously.

'Ye're looking a wee bit better this morn, Missie,' she lied gallantly, adding cautiously, 'nay doot ye'll be glad of y' breakfast.'

To her surprise the girl gave her a small wintry smile. 'Thank you, yes!'

Meg put a match to the open fire, laid quietly by Jock at seven, and then bustled back down to her kitchen. She knew that Glencurran was in the bathroom and she'd left the door ajar.

Even so, Ross only just caught the faint tinkle of what sounded like breaking china.

He covered the few yards to Nova's bedroom door in a second, and hurled himself like a jungle cat across the intervening space, to stop short at the bedside as Nova raised startled, questioning eyes. After a long moment's pause, he dropped his gaze to survey the shattered breakfast plate and two pieces of thin toast which lay on the rug beside the big bed.

'I'm s-so sorry,' Nova began nervously. 'It slipped off the tray and hit the cabinet handle. I h-hope it wasn't a valuable set?'

Glencurran was so relieved that his terrible fear had been groundless that he sought to cover his emotion with anger.

'You really are a very poor guest,' he stated coldly. 'Not content with running my staff off their feet for nothing, you smash up my best china!'

It was unforgivably rude, and Nova responded instantly in a way that filled her tormentor with secret delight. The pale face flamed with brief humiliation. 'I shall, of course, pay for any damages I may inflict during my unwilling stay here—and,' she took a deep breath, 'I shall leave you and your horrid house just as soon as I can!'

She spoke in a tense, quiet voice, but the violet-blue eyes literally sparked with anger and—was it unshed tears?

Pride, which Nova had not felt for a long time, forced her to hold back the tears, but to Ross's great satisfaction, she suddenly snatched up the empty breakfast cup and hurled it furiously across the room, where it shattered against the wardrobe.

'You can add that to my bill,' the girl stated icily.

'Oh, I will! And I'll take payment for both—now!' Ross bent swiftly to grip the slender wrists, forcing them down and backwards; then, delighted at this opportunity to keep the newly roused fighting spirit inflamed he pressed a rough, demanding kiss on to Nova's trembling lips.

When he released her, she sank back weakly against her pillows. But the look she gave Glencurran spoke volumes; a look that gave him a qualm of unease, speaking as it did of outraged pride, fear—and intense dislike.

'God,' he thought ruefully, 'I don't want *that* look to become a habit. Must strike a happy medium somehow. As soon as possible, too!' He turned away from the bedside as Meg tapped anxiously at the door, entering at his order.

'Come away in, Meggie,' he said easily. 'Miss Nova's had a smashing time. Got your pan and brush handy?' And with an outrageous grin he left a gaping Meg Graham to clear up the broken china.

Chapter Seven

It was on that morning and indeed, at that moment, that Nova began reforming her ideas. After a light breakfast, Meg had helped her across to the bathroom, and supervised her toilet with motherly concern, which reminded her of her longing for Lossie.

She slept dreamlessly until twelve and awoke really refreshed, to look around at the pleasant room. It wasn't really cold, but the fire looked good. Soft muslin curtains billowed gently, as a fresh September breeze passed gaily by the open window.

Nova suddenly felt a sense of well being; almost a sense of being glad to be alive and thinking of facing the world again. The sky beyond the big window, showed clear and bright . . . Where *was* she? 'I'll ask that very kind Meg,' she thought, and knew a little feeling of shame at the trouble she must have been to such a kindly considerate person.

'I must ask the name of that odious man too,' she murmured aloud.

She did so when Meg entered with lunch a short while later.

Meg, delighted in the girl's interest at last, was only too happy to oblige.

'Yon's Ross Glencurran. He owns a castle on Loch Curra in Inverness; three farms; two or three guest houses; eleven hundred acres; his own flock of special breed sheep, and a small tweed factory on the outskirts of Fort Augustus.

'He also owns this island.' She paused for breath as Nova's eyes opened with startled attention. The list had infuriated her, but the last . . .! Then she remembered her host's last remark . . .

'An island! Am I really on an island?' she gasped. There was no mistaking the horror in her voice.

'Och ay! It's only small, ye ken! Aboot one and a half miles long and just over half a mile wide. It's called Curransay and it's in Loch Sunart. Glenbeg is aboot four hundred yards awa—across the loch! Oronsay's about a mile away on t'other side. This hoose were built by Mr Ross's grandaddy, ye ken, an' Mr Ross comes here for six weeks every September.'

Meg rambled on happily enough now that her young charge seemed so much more normal . . .

She couldn't know that Nova was building up a great resentment and dislike of the autocratic man who had forced her away from her first dreadful idea of letting go.

'Er—how do you all get to and from the island?' she asked curiously.

'Boss has a cruiser. The *Heather*, named after his mither, who died about five years ago. Don't ye remember the boat at all?'

Meg queried.

'I believe I do,' Nova told her in a soft voice. 'It was taking off from—was it here?—when I arrived at Ardslignish.'

She dropped her eyes quickly then and bit her lip; looking up again immediately as the man she now knew to be Ross Glencurran, entered the room after a peremptory knock on the door.

He threw Meg Graham a quick smile and strolled towards the bed. He handed the girl two thick envelopes. 'Mail for you, Miss Helmann. Jock's just back from Glenbeg. Couple for you downstairs, Meg,' he said easily, and dropped into a chair nearby.

'Why—how—how does anyone know I am here?' Nova asked, her eyes wide.

Meg hastily left the room and he waited until she'd clumped, somewhat heavily, downstairs before answering.

'I'll tell you, then you can read your letters. Your friend Sara happens to be a neighbour of mine, more or less! She wrote asking me for Lossie's address, not knowing that I would be so close to my old nurse. I phoned them both on Tuesday morning. Those who love you have been pretty concerned.' He said it coldly, and Nova flinched.

'Aren't you going to read me a lecture on the cowardliness of my action?'

'No! It takes a great deal of rather desperate courage to decide to end it all at your age.' His eyes held hers with a certain arrogance. 'It will take even more courage for you to give me any further trouble in that direction,' he added cruelly, 'so don't try it.'

A wave of humiliation sent the hot anger rushing to Nova's head. How dare he make her feel like an idiot child!

'I shan't trouble you for your unwilling hospitality much longer,' she said between small clenched teeth. 'I shall get up now and should be grateful if your—your man would kindly run me back to Ardslig—'

'I don't think so,' he interrupted her. You see I promised Lossie I'd—er—take care of you, at least until she returns! That won't be for at least two more weeks, so I'm afraid we shall have to endure each other for a while.'

His eyes met her stunned protest with a mocking gleam. 'Besides, had you forgotten that it was I who fished you out of the loch— and that your life is mine—to do with as *I* please?'

For a moment she surveyed him in shocked silence; the soft colour flooding her pale face. Then, 'Mr Glencurran! I *know* what I so nearly did was wrong and—and I should be very grateful to you . . . b-but my feelings are still a bit confused!' The soft voice shook a little, then she squared her slim shoulders. 'I hope one day I'll be brave enough to thank you *sincerely*. But just now I can only feel intense

53

dislike for you, and y-your horrid remark only urges me to want to get away from this p-place,—and you—as quickly as possible.' She drew a deep and quivering breath, adding firmly, 'As soon as I feel a bit stronger I hope you will be gentleman enough to let me go!'

He had flinched involuntarily at the 'intense dislike' bit, but now a spark of amusement lit his clear eyes and the strong mouth twitched.

'What a speech!' he gibed. 'I don't believe I'd like anybody who gave me bruises like these either!' He leaned down and took her small hands, gazing at the faint, blue marks, then touched a little bruise at the side of the sweetly curved mouth.

She closed her eyes obstinately at his nearness and did not see the sudden tenderness in his eyes.

'Tell you what,' he said softly, 'you take it easy for a few days, and get some colour in that pale face, and we'll talk about it. Meanwhile—let's call a truce.'

The misty eyes flew open and she regarded him briefly, tugging her hands from his huge grasp.

'All right,' she agreed at last—reluctantly. 'But I'm sure I'll be fit enough to get lodgings in Ardslignish until Miss Lossiemuir returns. I'll be better by tomorrow, at least!'

'We'll see! Now I'll leave you to read your mail.'

Nova lay thoughtfully for several moments. For the rust time she had really taken in the appearance of the man whom she was beginning to look upon as her gaoler. That he was big and very strong, she had been certainly aware, but now she recalled a strong, brown face, craggy rather than handsome; with good teeth, and those very hard, green-flecked eyes. His hair, thick and springing, was an unusual shade of dark, reddish brown, and would have been any woman's crowning glory. His age? Nova guessed it to be around thirty, (he was in fact thirty-four) but she remembered with a flinch that Steven was thirty-one.

With a deep sigh she turned to her letters.

Lossie's was full of loving concern and deep regret that her sister's accident had called her away at just the wrong time. She urged Nova to be a good lassie; to stay put and let Meg Graham build her up again and to write to her at once.

Sara's was similar, but Nova felt shame and guilt flood her face as she read of their fright and concern. The letter went on, 'How strange that your old nurse should be living so near to Ross Glencurran's little island! We were so relieved, Uncle Miles and I, to hear from him that you are safe; you couldn't be in better hands,'—Nova made an irritable gesture—were they *all* on his side? 'I am going back to my home on Friday, dear Nova, and may be able to come and see you. I'll write again soon.

By the way, since the news of your broken engagement got about, one or two of your 'trendy' friends have expressed sympathy, and S.B. has been coldly received by your mother's old acquaintances *and* ourselves!'

Nova felt a pang at her friend's reference to Steven Blanchard, but felt at last a little flame of anger at his treachery.

A small smile dimpled the bruised mouth briefly at Sara's remark re her 'trendy' friends. A few 'way out' types had enjoyed browsing in the antique shop; mostly students, and she had become quite pally with one or two.

She had felt herself abandoned and alone, now, suddenly, it was good to know that one still had friends; even if the longing was still for someone really close, someone to love and to lean on.

When Meg entered the room at four o'clock, Nova was sitting by the fire, engrossed in writing answers to her mail.

She raised a heat-flushed face to the older woman's pleased smile, returning it with a sweet one of her own.

'Will you stay and have tea with me, please Meg?' she asked diffidently, and was very pleased when her invitation was accepted.

'I'll just away and get some more goodies,' Meg said pleasantly.

Nova finished her letters, and did full justice to the 'tea time goodies'. Now it was of the utmost importance that she build up her strength—because she had decided to get off the island—somehow . . . !

Nova was prepared to fight!

Chapter Eight

For the first time in a long while, Nova had slept dreamlessly, waking only when Meg knocked with morning tea.

Her drawing of the heavy curtains revealed a pale blue, clean-washed sky, very welcome after the soft drizzle that had persisted throughout the night.

'What a lovely morning, Mrs Graham,' she said—and meant it.

'Och! September is ay a bonny month,' Meg returned gladly. 'I'll be sorry to see it pass. The following Sunday is October first, d'ye ken?'

'Yes! I've been here six days,' Nova flushed a little, then continued, 'I—I'll be quite able to go back to the mainland in a day or two.'

Meg made no comment, only threw her a slow smile.

When she left Nova a few moments later, it was with the girl's cheerful insistence that 'I'll be *down* to breakfast in about half an hour, thank you!'

It was a little less when Nova made her way to the foot of the wide shallow stairs and stood hesitating, unsure of her direction. The clink of china from the half open door to the back of the side hall, gave her a lead, and she went towards it, calling, 'Mrs Graham? May I please come in?' She put her head cautiously round

58

the door.

'Good morning, Miss Helmann! Nice to see you actually tracking "down the grub." Did you follow your pretty little nose?' The deep voice was mocking, but the hazel eyes met hers keenly, as Ross left his seat to draw out a chair beside his and motioned her to be seated.

Nova coloured a little as she met that glance, but she gave him a cool smile, and took the proffered chair. 'No—just the sound of crocks!'

She allowed Glencurran to pile her plate, and tucked into an extremely hearty breakfast.

When he rose to what she estimated must have been over six feet, it was to inform her that he'd like to show her around this end of Curransay after lunch and after a tiny hesitation she accepted.

But he hadn't missed the tiny flame of excitement in her eyes and grinned to himself.

Nova endeared herself completely to Meg Graham, by helping to clear the table, wash up and then tackle a bowl of potatoes, taking a lively interest in the big cheerful kitchen as she worked.

The cooker was a big, four burner, Valor range, the normal sized oven using two of them. It had a long rack beneath and was supplied with oil from a big inverted bottle. She learned that the house, built by Ross's grandfather, had eight rooms, two bathrooms, and solid fuel central heating.

'How about ironing?' she asked, genuinely intrigued. Meg explained the beautiful oil heated Tilley she used, and added that there were also three old-fashioned 'flatties'. She also had a huge modern version of the old-fashioned dolly tub of which she was very proud.

'It's ay a verra comfortable hoose ye ken,' she told Nova with a deep laugh. 'I'll show ye round in a bit, then we'll hae coffee.'

Half an hour later Nova followed her on the 'grand tour'. The Grahams' bed-sitting-room had at one time been the master bedroom, with its own small bathroom. There were two other big rooms, one square, like the one Nova was using now and the other, which was Glencurran's, at the far end of the wide landing, long and spacious.

Back on the ground floor, Nova exclaimed in delight at the pleasant sitting-room, directly beneath her host's bedroom. The fire was already laid in a big open hearth and the room was light, with vivid orange and brown furnishings. The entire house was lit by Aladdin and Tilley lamps.

Certainly the master of Castle Glencurran knew how to make himself comfortable, even on a remote island! Nova drew a deep breath.

'It's a very nice house; so solid and—er—quite unexpected!'

'Ay! These islands rarely hae more than a few wee cottages on 'em, forbye,' Meg agreed.

'Mr Ross has repaired three on 'em at the far end. Used to be occupied a hundred years or so ago, but his granddaddy left 'em empty.'

Nova was shown into another, smaller, sitting-room, then the dining-room and so back to the cheerful kitchen.

'Doesn't it get very lonely for you and Mr Graham?'

'Weel—no! Ye see, Mr Ross lets all his friends, the family, and also the staff use it from end o' March 'till end of August. Then o'course he comes himsel' from first week in September to end of October ye ken. Jock and mesel' we stay on 'till end of November, to gi'e the hoose a good clean oop, then tis off to Oban for us. We've a wee cottage there and a married daughter close by. We dinna return till the end of February.'

'Oh my! That doesn't sound as though you have any *time* to get lonely. Does Mr Glencurran allow everyone to use his boat as well?'

'He does that! There's a fair-sized row-boat too.' Meg turned away and missed the thoughtful gleam that entered the girl's eyes.

Whilst Meg put the finishing touches to lunch, Nova went outside. The house stood on a flat plateau some sixty feet above, and about one hundred feet back, from a small curving beach. Looking down and to her right, she could see the two men busily packing up their tools preparatory to returning for lunch, and

61

her eyes went to the little stone jetty at the end of which a thirty foot cabin cruiser swayed gently on the sparkling waters of the loch.

About four hundred yards away across the water, Nova could see several grey stone cottages grouped together and a tiny church. This must be Glenbeg she surmised correctly. There were trees everywhere; the glorious shades of autumn already staining the slopes with vivid colour.

Indeed, so glorious were the colours of a great stretch of forest beyond the village, that Nova gasped at its beauty. She was to learn that this was Glen Borrodale but now, her vision was caught again by the movements of the men as they strolled up a gently sloping path and finally on to a wide path fronting the house.

'Hello! Admiring the view?' Glencurran queried coolly as he approached.

'Well—yes! I'd no idea it was so breath-takingly beautiful,' Nova answered honestly.

His eyes dwelt on her appreciatively for a moment. She had on a vivid scarlet jersey, with pale grey tweed slacks, and a scarlet ribbon held the beautiful, blue-black hair from the small face. Her ivory skin had a faint colour today, and the hollow look wasn't so pronounced. The violet-blue eyes met his for a moment, before the long silky lashes fell to hide her sudden confusion.

'Glad you like it,' he uttered laconically, 'but

the view isn't the only beautiful thing around here.' And he took her arm and led her back to the kitchen.

When lunch was over, Nova again helped to clear, and then Meg and Jock set off across to Glenbeg, and the Conways' store to pick up supplies. Meg had been well briefed on what to say and managed to answer all kindly enquiries without once resorting to lies.

Nova had stood at the front door, watching them go a little wistfully, and the man lighting his pipe a few feet away, frowned.

'Go and change your shoes,' he ordered curtly. 'Those sandals won't do beyond the garden.'

Nova's chin lifted proudly but she turned to obey. 'After all,' she thought eagerly, 'if I am to get away, I have to find out all I can about the place . . .'

He took her along a narrow track that wound to the top of the hill, and she looked back to see the house, on its sheltered plateau, some seventy feet below them. She followed him steadily for over half a mile, finally stopping at the top of a small rise from which she turned to gaze. Following his pointing finger, the far end of the island faced towards the Sound of Mull; to the right the Isle of Oronsay; to the near end, down the length of Loch Sunart, and coming full circle, back to the house facing Glenbeg.

'There are three cottages a little further on,'

he told her. 'We'll go right to that end tomorrow; it's only a mile and a quarter.'

Nova sat down on a rock and rubbed her foot. She was wearing small walking shoes; unfortunately the ones Meg had dried out for her, and their resultant stiffness had made them very uncomfortable.

'I don't think I could have made it today,' she admitted, 'but I'll hunt out my other low-heeled casuals tomorrow.'

He dropped to one knee and took the small foot in his hand, easing off the shoe. He then proceeded to press and bend it until it became more pliable. Slipping it back on he tackled the other one.

'Try 'em now,' he demanded, and because instant obedience seemed to be becoming a habit, she did so, walking up and down.

'That's a *lot* better—thank you!' she smiled, genuinely grateful. 'One can see water on all sides,' she added inconsequentially, waving her hand around. 'It really *is* an island, isn't it?'

'Er—yes!' and because he couldn't keep the laughter out of his eyes, she was reminded of her determination to best him. Her own grew frosty, and she turned to retrace her steps, ignoring the large brown hand held out to assist her over the rough spots.

She was startled to discover that she was to dine alone with Glencurran that evening and questioned Meg about it.

That good lady told her that this was always

so for Ross. Breakfast and lunch in the kitchen; dinner alone or with guests if any, after which she and Jock went to their own bed-sitting-room for the night.

'Mr Ross gets his own supper, ye ken,' she informed Nova.

So, defiantly refusing to change, she joined her host reluctantly for the evening. It turned out better than she'd expected, as Glencurran had a wonderful selection of records.

She didn't remember the moment when, lulled by the serene beauty of *Clair de Lune*, she dropped off to sleep. She murmured drowsy protest as Glencurran lifted her with consummate ease, and carried her aloft; here to lay her gently down, and to touch a light kiss to her closed eyes before seeking Meg to help his unwilling guest to bed . . .

Chapter Nine

Nova woke the following morning to find the tiny island cut off apparently, from the rest of the world, by a thick white mist.

Jock explained to her that this was a natural come back, from two days sun following steady rain.

' 'Twill be gone by midday,' he assured her.

He proved to be right and Nova couldn't quite believe her good luck when Ross Glencurran offered to take her to the far end of Curransay in the *Heather* after lunch. If he was aware of her intention of noting the possibilities of getting off the island by boat, he gave no sign of it in the casual smile he threw her as he tackled a hearty meal.

They set off just after two, Glencurran assuring Jock that they'd be back by six.

'He and Meg are to spend the evening with the Conways, so we shall have the pleasure of a tinned dinner tonight!' he warned her.

Nova felt her spirits sink at the thought of being alone with her tough host for an entire evening. Then she cheered up. It wouldn't be much longer and she mustn't let him see her eagerness to be gone.

'Perhaps I can hustle us up a meal of sorts,' she offered, 'if Meg won't mind. I'd enjoy it.'

'Meg worries herself witless when she leaves

me to cope! She'll be delighted,' he uttered satirically, adding, 'Actually tho', I'm a fair cook! But a meal prepared by your own fair hands will be very welcome!'

His eyes laughed down at her face, noting the little spark of temper that flashed briefly in her eyes.

'If you are able to cope so well then you won't need my help, will you?' she retorted proudly, and ran lightly down the little path towards the jetty.

Still smiling, he followed in his unhurried way; his long strides covering the ground almost as quickly as Nova's small, running steps.

Nova forgot her annoyance as Glencurran showed her over the boat.

It was trim and sparkling with white paint. He lifted her down into the cockpit, then led her through into a roomy saloon. This was well equipped with upholstered seats that he told her were single bunks on occasion, and a formica covered table. Under seat lockers, shelves and gay curtains completed the pleasant interior.

He showed her the little two berth cabin, at the aft end, then back through the saloon and cockpit, down three steps to a little galley.

'A tiny bathroom and toilet completes the tour,' he told her, waving a big hand at the narrow door to one side.

'It's beautiful! So comfortable and well

equipped! You must have a lot of fun in it!' She gazed around with delight and genuine interest.

'I enjoy using it—yes! Come on, let's get off, or we'll be late back,' and he motioned her back to the cockpit, where she scrambled on to the wide seat beside him.

He was fully aware that she watched his actions intently, as he handled the boat expertly away from the jetty and his mouth quirked.

He began pointing out various places as they ran past the tip of Curransay.

'The colourful stretch of forest to your right on the mainland is Glen Borrodale,' he told her, 'and the large island out ahead of us is Oronsay. Have you never been this way before, Nova?'

'N-no! I have been to Glasgow a couple of times—when Mother was alive. She had an old friend there.' She turned towards him, 'I am completely stunned by the beauty of all this, though! And the air is like—like—wine, isn't it?' She drew in a great breath and suddenly realised how *very* glad she was to be alive.

'Yes! It's good and clean. I hope it will always remain so!' His tone was unusually sombre, and Nova guessed him to be thinking of the air pollution that was creeping around this wonderful planet like an evil veil. For a brief moment the violet eyes met the hazel ones in complete sympathy and understanding.

Then, remembering that she almost hated this big, strong man, Nova looked away.

She noted with interest, that two or three cabin cruisers, looking like toys at this distance, were moving up and down in the tiny bays.

Some fifteen minutes later, Glencurran tied up at another tiny stone jetty and assisted Nova out of the cockpit.

'I hope your shoes are okay this time?' he said, with a glance at the little suede casuals she wore. Their russet brown toned exactly with the slacks she wore, and a vivid orange jumper made a warm contrast.

'Oh yes!' she laughed. 'I've stuffed the others with newspaper to stretch them again.' Her face flooded with colour. 'Do we have far to walk?'

'The cottages are only about three hundred feet from here. Look! See them in that stand of trees?'

She followed his pointing finger and saw the picturesque group, huddling near each other as though for company, but when they drew near, after a scramble up a rocky path, she saw that each sturdy little 'bothy' had its own small plot enclosed by low stone walls.

The inside of each one was a great surprise. Ross and Jock had painted all the interiors in bright, clean colours, added shelves and small cupboard units, and in one corner of each long living-room, partitioned off little 'kitchen' areas. In each case a tiny outhouse had been converted to a bathroom.

The floors, mostly stone, were in a shocking mess of dust and paint splashes.

'Oh dear! That's going to be a job for someone,' Nova opined ruefully, 'but the work you've done is great! Did it take you long?'

'Nearly three years! Due to the fact that I wouldn't let Jock do any of the work until I arrived each year!'

'What will you do with them?' Nova asked curiously.

'I've had to refuse some of the staff when they've asked for holidays on the island,' he told her calmly. 'Meg and I will come up soon, give 'em a good clean up, and hang curtains. Then I'll furnish them as holiday cottages— for my own staff only! I've no intention of turning my island into a holiday camp!' There was a note of aggressive possession in his deep voice, a note of deeply rooted pride of heritage . . .

The girl threw him a nervous look over her shoulder. 'I can't see you in the role of "Mrs Mopp",' she laughed then.

'You'd be surprised,' he answered coolly. 'I'm pretty handy at most things I set my mind to.'

The mockery was back in his eyes and the white teeth gleamed in his brown, weather-beaten face.

Nova's lashes dropped, and she glanced

hastily at her wrist-watch. 'Is—is it time we started back?' she asked, and he laughed, understanding at once her unspoken physical unease of him.

'Not yet. Meg put up a wee hamper for us. We'll have tea up on the point. It's only a short way from here. You'll like it! It looks out towards the Sound of Mull. Come on.' And he led the way out, turning to lock the door behind him.

'One never knows,' he said satirically, answering the unspoken question in Nova's surprised eyes.

She waited at the top of the path whilst he returned to collect the little hamper, and together they continued to the top of a fairly steep rise. From here, it was something of a scramble to the top of a shrub covered bluff but the view from it was wonderful.

Nova stood panting; the cool late September breeze lifting her glossy hair back from a face glowing from her exertions. Suddenly her eyes caught sight of a large cabin cruiser heading past the tip of the island, some two hundred feet away. Without a second's thought, she ran towards the edge of the bluff, high above the little beach, her arms raised to attract attention.

'Hey! Hey!' she yelled shrilly, at the top of her voice, her arms waving frantically.

The man at the wheel of the cruiser didn't hear her cry, as the wind was against her, but he thought he saw a flash of brilliant colour up on the point of Curransay. But his searching eyes found nothing and he shook a puzzled head.

Glencurran had hurled himself at the slight figure before she had taken more than a few steps away from him and thrown her down behind the thickly clumped shrubs in the middle of her last yell. Her breath was knocked out of her completely as his weight was thrown across her, and then his powerful hand clamped itself across her mouth stifling the frantic scream.

He held her thus, completely helpless, for several long moments, his eyes blazing down into the wide, tear-filled ones beneath him.

She tried to push his weight away with small shaking hands, but he merely gathered her wrists in his other hand and gave a cruel little smile, shaking his head.

'Be still, little Nova,' he whispered coldly, and raised his head to peer between the bushes.

The cabin cruiser had headed towards Mull, and was well away from them by now. Its occupant, with his back to Curransay, had already forgotten that which he had only half seen . . .

Waiting only long enough to scan the water in all directions, the owner of Curransay returned his bleak gaze to the girl's. Then he removed his hand, already wet with tears, from the soft mouth, leaving angry finger marks on the rounded jaw.

A strange look crossed his craggy face as he sat up on the thick turf, and lifted the shaken Nova into his arms, rocking her gently.

'Nova! Nova! What a silly thing to do,' he uttered sternly. 'Do you want to make all the front page headlines again?'

At the mention of 'headlines' Nova had gone still; then, after a long pause, she let her soft weight sink against him and began to fumble for her handkerchief. He pressed his into her hand and waited patiently while she mopped up.

'No! No! It was an impulse, Mr Glencurran! Now that you've pointed out the possible results of s-such an action, I'm g-glad it didn't c-come off!' She drew a shuddering breath and raised her still frightened eyes, the lashes spiky and wet, to his. 'You d-didn't need to be so— so *rough*!' she said reproachfully.

He tipped up her chin in relentless fingers. 'Are you telling me that I could have stopped you any other way?' he said evenly. 'I think not, Nova!' His eyes softened a little at her shamed face. 'Look! Let's forget it, eh? We'll enjoy tea, and perhaps you'll be a good girl and try to tolerate me until Lossie comes back. I'm quite kind really!' His tone was so lugubrious, that Nova gave a shaky and unwilling laugh.

'All right!' she conceded, with a final deep

sigh. 'Just one more thing,' she added in a small, appealing voice. 'Would it have caused trouble if I'd managed to escape to Glenbeg?'

'Such an unwilling prisoner!' he mocked. 'No! I don't think so, Nova! Everyone over there thinks that you were taking a walk when Jock and I saw you keel over in a faint, so we landed to help you. You—er—graciously accepted my offer of hospitality on the basis of our mutual nurse. No one knows of your mishap but myself, the Grahams, Lossie and Sara. Not *even* Miles Tremayne! OK?' His eyes dominated her until she relaxed, then he released her and began unpacking the hamper. Nova felt a strange reluctance to leave his arms.

'Come on!' he smiled. 'Let's eat! I'm starving!'

This was so normal that Nova had no choice but to respond but she remained a little subdued throughout the rest of the evening. Only towards bedtime, her chaotic thoughts in order after much confused heart-searching, did she come to realise just how much she owed to Ross Glencurran's powerful personality. She felt stirred by him as never with Blanchard—reluctantly . . .

Just after nine o'clock, their dinner finished, she met his eyes with a strange awareness . . .

'Thank you,' she whispered, 'thank you for *everything,* Mr Glencurran!'

'Any time!' and he stooped to press a kiss to

74

the corner of her mouth.

'*Now, now,*' he thought to himself exultantly, 'I *might* get somewhere!'

Chapter Ten

Nova drank in the beauty and peace of her surroundings with an eagerness that surprised herself. Now, her clear bell-like laughter was heard often in the solid stone house, bringing a leap of the pulses to Glencurran whenever he shared it.

Her attitude towards him had vastly improved but he knew that she was still nervous of him—naturally so. Hadn't he imposed his domination on her shocked and failing senses in no uncertain manner? He was to very nearly regret the hidden reserves of strength and pride he had aroused . . .

His statement that her life now belonged to him had had its desired effect. She was grateful, but determined to prove now that no man was her keeper; that she was quite capable of managing her own life.

Glencurran could only hope that having succeeded in rousing her fighting spirit, along with hearty dislike for himself, he would now gradually be able to replace it with the spark of love, deep though it might be hidden. He couldn't know that Nova also was fighting a physical response to him.

Hadn't Sara assured him that Nova had never yet been really in love? His eyes held a red gleam as they followed the girl's slim, shapely figure, where she scrambled ahead of him to the top of the bluff near the cottages.

'Careful,' he warned, as a little shower of loose scree spun from beneath the small feet.

They had come over with Meg to start on the clean up of the little bothies, and the lunch break over, Nova had asked if she might come up here for a breath of air.

There was certainly plenty of it up here! For the past two days a lively breeze had whipped across the Sound tossing the blue-grey waters, and sending showers of red and gold leaves scurrying wildly.

It caught at Nova now as Glencurran came up beside her, and she swayed, clinging to him as he placed a steadying arm around her. She drew herself gently away, but retained a grip on his leather coat pocket for safety.

'Is that Ardslignish over there?' she asked breathlessly, pointing to the little wooden jetty and a few roof tops some five hundred yards away across the water.

'That's right. We were making for the jetty down below,' he nodded to the little beach beneath them, 'when I first caught sight of you.' He said it casually, but Nova flushed, and turned to gaze away across the sparkling waters. A deep sigh left her parted lips.

'It's all so beautiful! I shall hate to leave it now,' she said wistfully. 'Lossie will be back this weekend so I shall stay with her for a few weeks—then—then I suppose I must go back and—face up to things.'

Ross turned her to face him, a hand beneath her chin. 'I'd say you've done all the facing up necessary these last days! All you need to do now, is to go on from here. I've a few ideas you may be interested in! We'll talk about 'em later!'

Nova laughed uncertainly before pulling herself firmly away, which with an inner, rueful smile he allowed her to do.

'Sounds intriguing,' she said, reserved again.

That evening after dinner, Ross gave her the box of chocolates purchased days ago at Conways', and taught her to play cribbage. He also told her that Sara and his cousin Ian were driving over from Kinlochleven at the end of her first week back with Lossie.

Nova was delighted. Sara had hinted in her own letters but no certain date had been mentioned. However, that night she again had the horrible dream of the closed door and the voice—a familiar one?—demanding that she enter the room she so feared.

The following day was Thursday and Meg, anxious to do a little more cleaning at the cottages, accepted Nova's offer to take over at the house, and set off cheerfully with her employer.

By ten o'clock, the overcast sky had cleared to a limpid autumn blue so Nova gladly agreed to pack a lunch and spend the rest of the morning helping Jock give the *Heather* a good clean out.

They stopped at one o'clock and Nova discovered she had forgotten the flask of coffee. 'I'll run back and get it. It won't take a moment!' she laughed, and sped lightly up the shallow slope.

Jock, waiting for her, walked back to the land end of the jetty to get his old pipe from his jacket, which was hanging on a small post. Even the most careful of us have mishaps and thus it was, that the sturdy, slow-moving Jock put his heavy boot in a patch of wet weed, and felt his legs fly from under him.

Nova, already half-way down, heard his sharp cry and saw him fall heavily; to lie still with outflung arms. She felt her heart leap with terror and went towards him with shaking limbs. Kneeling down, she leaned over him and touched the side of his face turned uppermost. Then she tried gently to turn him on his back but the next moment recoiled in horror. The other side of Jock's face was covered in blood. Her fingers were covered with it, and with her senses reeling, she staggered to her feet and flew back towards the house, her one thought, to get away from that terrible sight . . .

Her hysterical headlong flight was cut short by a grip of iron. She raised shocked and panic stricken eyes to the fury of Glencurran's icy look. His grip was painful and he shook her sharply.

'Pull yourself together, you little fool!' he ordered harshly. 'I can see Jock's had an accident and we'll need you to help. Now come on, stop it!' And he shook her roughly again.

Nova gave a sobbing moan. 'Oh don't—*please, please,*' she begged. 'I can't look at him! I can't! My father—my father—' She shuddered and closed her eyes, and then he remembered that Nova had been the one to find Charles Helmann, with the side of his head reduced to a bleeding pulp. A great tide of pity and tenderness swept over him but he knew this thing had to be conquered *now*—or maybe never—so he hardened his heart.

'Look Nova, blood only means *someone* is hurt and in pain! *Never,* never run from it. You may be able to save a life, or at least assuage pain. Jock needs us, and we are wasting time with your cowardice,' he added brutally. Taking her wrist, he tugged her after him, back along the last few yards to where Jock still lay senseless.

He quickly made a pad of his jacket and lifted the injured man's head on to it gently. Then he began to mop the face clean, soon soaking his large handkerchief. He turned to the white-faced girl he had dragged down beside him. 'What've you got, Nova?' ignoring her almost fainting condition. 'I need more linen, hankies will do. See what you have in your jacket pockets,' he ordered brusquely and urgently.

At that moment Jock gave a deep groan, moving his head slightly and the girl made a visible effort to control her quivering nerves.

She rummaged in her pockets and produced three small hankies and a small packet of tissues which she held out to Ross speechlessly.

His hard eyes met hers. 'You do it,' he ordered curtly, 'while I get the first aid kit from the boat,' and he rose swiftly.

Jock moaned again and his eyes opened heavily, only to close again instantly. Suddenly . . . Nova's ghost was laid.

'Oh! poor Jock!' she said, and moving closer, began to press a thick wad of tissues over the side of his face.

'It's still bleeding a lot,' she told Ross anxiously when he returned.

'Good girl,' he approved, surveying her handiwork. She said nothing, but leaned to take Jock's work-roughened hand in her small grasp and watched intently, as Ross applied a thicker, disinfected pad.

Fifteen minutes later they helped a groggy Jock on to the *Heather* and here a pale-faced Meg joined them.

'Thank the Guid Lord we'd decided to gang awa back hame early,' she uttered thankfully, 'tho, Mr Ross says ye were tending ma laddie verra well.' She gave Nova's hand a grateful squeeze, and then sat down cautiously by the recumbent Jock, who had managed a faint grin at the words 'ma laddie'. The grin reassured his anxious watchers greatly.

A short time later they were all in his big car heading for the cottage hospital at Salen. It was the first time in nearly three weeks that Nova had been off the island but somehow, she didn't even think about it . . .

After handing Jock over to a kindly and efficient staff, Ross took the two ladies—both looking a little wan—to a nearby tea shop and regaled them with really good, hot tea. Even the anxious Meg regained a little of her lost ruddy colour.

Nova, also refreshed, seemed to be in a remote dream world of her own. Later, as they waited to collect Jock, Glencurran heard her soft murmur of 'Poor Daddy, poor Daddy,' and knew that for the first time, pity and sorrow outweighed the horror and shock she had felt all those long, lost weeks ago. The eyes that met his as he grasped her hand to lead her back to the car, were unbearably sad but very serene and quietly hopeful.

They fussed over a bemused Jock, who had been given Tetanus injections, eleven stitches in the gash that ran from just beneath his eye to the bottom of his ear, and a good supply of tablets to ensure plenty of rest.

'See you in seven days, Mr Graham,' the matron reminded him and Glencurran headed the car back the nine miles to Glenbeg.

For the next two days Nova took over the

cooking completely, in order to give Meg all the time possible with a reluctant invalid. But on Sunday morning she bid them both a warm farewell, promising to come over as often as Ross would bring her and was swung into the cockpit on her way back to Rowan Cottage at last.

Lossie was overwhelmed with emotion when Ross took Nova in through the little back porch. He stood surveying them as they embraced tearfully, with a resigned cynicism.

'Well! If you two are going to keep this up for long—I can see there'll be no lunch forthcoming, so I'll just away!'

Lossie's sturdy Scot's common sense immediately asserted itself, and suddenly, to Nova, things became normal, as she heard Lossie tell the tough Glencurran, 'Behave now laddie. We had to greet a bit y' ken?'

'You know,' Nova told Glencurran, as she saw him off later, 'there are a few things I'd like to forget happened over there on Curransay but on the whole, it *was* rather nice! I'll miss it—and—and—all of you,' she ended breathlessly, not meeting his eyes.

He pulled her close within the tight circle of his arms. 'I'll be content if you just miss *me*,' he assured her coolly, 'and just to make *sure* that you don't *forget* me—' he bent his tall head, and took the startled lips in a deep and breath-taking kiss. Nova's heart lurched . . .

Then, with a brief salute, he swung aboard

the *Heather* leaving a stunned Nova wondering what had hit her. Her last wish was to fall in love with Ross. Pride alone forbade it—and yet—!

'Don't forget! I'll be over to take you to dinner on Tuesday,' he called back as the boat headed away towards the island.

Nova lifted a hand in acknowledgement and then returned to her beloved Lossie, suppressing the feeling of sudden emptiness that assailed her.

Chapter Eleven

For the first few days Nova allowed her old friend to fuss and mother her then, with a new strength of character, she gently insisted that it stopped.

'I am quite capable of making a fuss of *you*, Lossie! So put your feet up this morning and *I'll* do the beds, tidy around and then prepare lunch.' She laughed with the sheer enjoyment of feeling fit and young.

This was Tuesday, and without being fully aware of it, part of her inner excitement came from the fact that this evening the Laird of Glencurran was to take her out to dinner. She had not seen him since her return and reluctantly enough, found herself missing his dominant presence.

When he rat-tatted loudly on the cottage door, it made them both jump. Lossie, settled with her knitting before a good fire, twinkled up at his brown face as he entered to bid her 'hello' and 'goodbye' with a firm hug of her plump shoulders.

'We shan't be too late,' he told her. 'Ready Nova?' His keen hazel eyes dwelt on her appearance with an appreciative glow and she coloured faintly, remembering his farewell kiss. A sudden nervousness assailed her and she bent quickly to kiss Lossie's russet cheek.

Glencurran had seen the little tremor, so deliberately set out to put her at ease proving himself a charming and amusing host on such an occasion. Nova recalled that during those first few evenings spent in the lovely sitting-room on Curransay, he had been less charming and more watchful, leaving her to amuse herself whilst he worked at designs for tweed.

True, she had often caught a strange gleam in his eyes and he had been ever ready to answer any questions she put to him. One or two evenings she had even been allowed to try her own hand at design and had brought a folder of ideas, and coloured pens, with which to complete the started efforts, back to Rowan with her.

They had dinner at a lovely old inn at a place called Kilchoan. Over an excellent meal, in a warm and pleasant room, Glencurran told her of the terrible and bloody sea battle, waged between this spot and Ardmore Point by the Macleods and the Macleans, in the fifteenth century.

They were by the wide mullioned window, and he drew back the curtain, leaning over to point away across the sea, to where, on this clear, sharp night, she could see lights twinkling far away.

'The lights of Tobermory,' he told her, 'and over to your right, beyond Ardmore Point— the Atlantic Ocean!'

'It's all so wild and beautiful,' she smiled, genuine interest sparkling in the violet-blue eyes. 'I'm sure this historic coast must have a ruined castle somewhere?'

'It has,' he said laconically. 'Mingary Castle. Where James the Fourth held court somewhere around fourteen ninety something or other.' His eyes met hers and they laughed together.

When he returned her to Rowan just after ten, all her fears were at least subdued, and he wisely, but reluctantly, left it at that, giving her a comradely peck on the cheek when he left soon after. He wasn't to know that Nova had sternly hidden her disappointment . . .

During the following days Nova found herself devoting quite a lot of time to the tweed designs, and Lossie helped by insisting she have an oil heater in her bedroom. The weather was lovely just now with pale, blue days and sharp but unclouded nights.

By Friday afternoon a lively breeze betokened a change on the way. Glencurran, calling for Nova in his big car, felt his pulses leap at the picture she made, poised in the doorway of Rowan.

She wore brown, corded slacks, with a chunky knit pullover and hood in turquoise and white. Her face glowed with restored health; the clear eyes shining with excited anticipation at the thought of seeing Sara again.

'You're a sight for sore eyes,' he informed her carelessly, covering up his almost uncontrollable urge to crush her close, and to cover the smiling, rosy mouth with kisses.

Lossie, well muffled against the wind, saw them off, expressing the hope that rough weather wouldn't prevent them all getting back to the mainland on Sunday afternoon.

'Ay! I don't believe we shall be out of doors much for a day or two! Bye for now, take care! Come along, little Nova.' And taking her hand, he ran her down the path.

In spite of a moment's embarrassment— ignored by the warm-hearted Sara—Nova was delighted to have her very good friend's company again. She noted, however, a special serenity as she introduced the tall, dark young man, who turned from gripping Glencurran's shoulder to smile at her.

'This is Ian Clarke, Ross's cousin, Nova dear.'

'Hello—may I?—Nova! A pretty name for a very pretty person! We are two lucky men, to be having such charmers on hand for a whole weekend!' He enveloped Nova's small hand in a lean, brown one and met her shy smile with a wide, impertinent grin of his own.

'He's just trying to prove that the Irish don't have the edge on blarney, Nova,' Ross broke in coolly, 'so take it with a pinch of salt even though it happens to be true!'

Sara hadn't been to Curransay before, so

88

just about everything delighted her, even the choppy waters of the loch.

Later that evening, dinner over, the two men sat bringing each other up to date on business matters, and Sara gave Nova a brief description of her own home, and of Castle Glencurran.

'It's at the head of a tiny loch, only four miles long and about half a mile wide, but has the most glorious views! It has its own beach, and a fishing lodge about half a mile from the Castle. There's a tiny village, with its own kirk, about two miles away and my father, who is the doctor for that area, has his practice about five miles away, at Kinlochleven.'

'It sounds like a good place to be, Sara! But I doubt if I'll ever get—' Nova began.

'Funny you should say that,' Glencurran drawled, suddenly looming above her, 'Lossie and I were saying what a good idea if you returned with me on the twenty-seventh of October, and join in our Hallowe'en party at the Castle.'

Meeting the unspoken challenge of his eyes, Nova hesitated; but pressed by an eager Sara and teased by the smiling Ian, she said, 'Yes! all right—I'd love to come! Thank you for asking me,' and she raised her chin with a proud and revealing gesture.

'Great!' was all he said, the lowered eyes hiding the satisfaction he felt. She couldn't have stayed with Miss Lossiemuir for ever, and this had seemed a very good way of breaking the ice. He knew that left to herself, Nova, in spite of her returned courage, might have let time slip by.

The weekend passed all too quickly; rough winds kept them house-bound for most of Saturday, but by Sunday morning, the previously wild loch, presented an innocent, unruffled face to the world.

'Just like a woman,' Ross drawled, rousing in an indignant Nova, an unusual desire to thump him.

For Sara's benefit they ran over to Oronsay where they managed to get very good, milky coffee at an obliging farmhouse, before returning in high spirits to a good lunch. The girls helped Meg wash up whilst the men put their cases on board, then thanking the Grahams warmly, the visitors left on the return trip to Glenbeg.

Nova stood beside Glencurran as Ian spun his rather rakish car round expertly and set off on the return to Kinlochleven.

'Goodbye, darlings. See you on the twenty-seventh!' Sara's voice floated back on the cool air and the reminder gave Nova a strange little lift of excitement. It was a long, long time since she had been present at a party.

Glencurran stayed to tea at Lossie's insistence, after which he asked to be shown Nova's progress with the designs.

'I've only finished two,' she murmured shyly.

He studied them in silence for a moment, then rolling them carefully, slipped them into his suede jacket pocket.

Nova watched him breathlessly. 'Aren't they m-much good?'

'Oh yes! *Very* good indeed! You have quite a hidden talent there.' He surveyed her anxious face for a moment. 'Get on with the others, won't you? I shan't be seeing you for some days now, Nova. Jock and I have a few things which must be done before we leave the island for winter. I shall call for you at ten o'clock on the morning of the twenty-seventh, so be ready.'

The eyes that met his were half exasperated, half annoyed; and he gently cuffed her on the chin.

'Yes! It is an order! It's quite a run back to Loch Curra, so time is important! As to your designs—I'll have more to say later—perhaps.' His eyes teased her and she half smiled.

But as the time passed, Nova found herself disappointed that so many days were to elapse before she saw him again. Lossie noted her preoccupation and drew her own wise conclusions. 'Mr Ross is aye a deep one,' she told herself 'and if he had made up his mind to ha'e yon lassie—then that's what he'll do.'

In the middle of her last week at Rowan Cottage Nova received a letter from her solicitor stating that he could do with her signature on several papers, and that the town

91

house had been sold. She heaved a sigh and Agnes Lossiemuir looked up anxiously.

'Lossie, dear! I was hoping to find my way back to you after my weekend with Ross but it looks as though I *must* go back to London. Mr Balfour—father's solicitor—wants me to sign some documents. I'll phone my ex-employer. She was a friend of mother's—Miss Carstairs —remember?' And at Lossie's nod, 'She will put me up for a time. Perhaps—may I come back to you later, dear?' Anxiously . . .

'Of course ye may, if nothing changes your mind, ma bonny! I think I'll awa' to my sister's agin—for a while, ye ken!'

So Nova made her phone call to Eve Carstairs and Miss Lossiemuir left a letter with the Conways for Glencurran, begging a lift to Strontian.

On Friday, as arranged, Ross turned up prepared to take Lossie as far as her destination; looking forward to having Nova's company to himself for the rest of the trip.

In spite of an early mist, which lifted by ten-thirty, the day was clear and sharp. Nova was enthralled by the beauty of the lovely shore road along Loch Sunart.

She bid a slightly tearful goodbye to Lossie in Strontian, then, in face of Glencurran's obvious impatience, she gave her old friend a final hug, and allowed him to take her hand back to the car.

A last wave and the big car shot away,

leaving Nova feeling as though an unreal and dreamlike episode in her life had come to an end.

93

Chapter Twelve

Glencurran followed the road at a moderate pace, in order to allow Nova time to soak in the early autumn beauty of the passing scenery. From time to time the man threw a quick glance at the vivid face alight with interest.

A little before one Glencurran spun the car into the parking area of Ardgour Hotel, where he seemed to be well known. They were shown to a table and spent a very pleasant hour over an extremely good lunch.

'We cross on the Corran ferry here, over to the other side of Loch Linnhe, to Onich. Then it's the road to home,' he told her with a smile; adding with a lift of the strong dark eyebrows, 'I wonder what you'll think of it?'

She couldn't know how important it was to him. It simply didn't occur to her that Glencurran's feelings could be deeply involved.

'Well—I have a feeling that it will be as stunning as any fairy-tale castle,' she teased.

'So it might be, but I can assure you that central heating helps a lot,' he replied cynically enough.

As they entered the road through Mamore Forest over an hour later, Nova caught sight of a stag, outlined against the sky and excitedly begged Ross to stop.

'Oh, Ross, please! Just for a moment,' and with a thrill that she had at last used his Christian name, impulsively and naturally, he drew up and leaned across to wind down the window for her. Through all these weeks, she had somehow always managed to avoid using his given name.

As Ross leaned with her to peer at the magnificent beast, already poised for flight, the delicious fragrance of a light perfume came to him and for a moment he nearly threw caution to the winds.

He grew suddenly curt as he wound up the window with a brief remark 'that she would probably see others from the Castle,' and Nova, feeling slightly rebuffed, sat back in silence as he jabbed the starter, and the car leapt forward.

Half an hour later they turned off a wide, unmade road that bordered a little loch, between great iron gates, onto a curving drive to end finally at a flight of shallow steps leading to a massive arched doorway.

Nova stood at the bottom of the steps with a slightly unreal feeling, rather as though she were caught in the pages of a *Scott* novel.

Glencurran, his eyes on her bemused face, stepped forward and drew her into his arms, raising her face with strong fingers. 'Welcome to my home, Nova,' and he kissed her lightly on the temple.

Nova blushed a little, but took this as a sign that they were friends again. 'Thank you,' she said shyly. 'It really is a fairy-tale castle, isn't it?'

A stocky, smiling man had already thrown open the door, and was now helping another man with their cases as Glencurran led her into the hall.

'Hello, you two! Nice to see you safely back! Just in time, too! It's going to be misty later on.'

'Ian! What are you doing here, and where's Jane?' Glencurran greeted his cousin.

'I'm here, sir! Ye'll be wantin' me tae show the young lady tae her room, nay doot?' Nova turned to face the tall, smiling woman who approached through a door to their left.

'Please. Nova, this is my housekeeper, Mrs Jane Murray. That's her husband James just coming in with your cases. Young Ginger behind him.' His eyes watched her alertly. It was going to be something of an ordeal he guessed, meeting so many strange people. He tensed as Nova made a small nervous gesture, then, in response to Jane Murray's smile, she stepped forward, holding out her hand shyly.

'Hello, Mrs Murray, Mr Murray,' with a nod in his direction—' and er—Ginger—may I?'

On a very relaxed note, Nova followed Mrs Murray up the beautifully carved staircase; along a wide, softly carpeted hallway, to a large, but somehow cosy room cheerful with

96

flickering firelight.

'Oh, how lovely! Thank you, Mrs Murray.'

Jane Murray eyed her kindly. She hadn't missed the little tremor downstairs, or the master's tight jaw as he'd watched her. 'Ye've a wee bathroom to yersel' through yon door— and tea will be ready in aboot fifteen minutes. The door I came oot of earlier, ye ken?'

She threw the girl another kindly smile and left.

The Scots, like the rest of the British people, do have a deep reserve but there are none kinder when their sympathies are aroused.

It needed only a quiet and confidential statement from the Laird of Glencurran to the effect that Miss Helmann had had a tragic loss, and had been very ill, for his entire staff to unobtrusively make a fuss of her.

Ian had brought over his sister Fiona to welcome her cousin and his young guest that first day, and Nova, shy at first, had soon responded warmly to the quiet charm of the older girl. She seemed to be very fond of Ross and briefly, Nova had wondered. The open Fiona had soon made things clear.

'I am engaged to marry Bruce Robson, tenant of Ross's biggest farm. You will meet him later. Ian, of course, manages the home farm; then there is one other tenanted by Joe Macdonald's son Rory.' She had laughed at the wideness of Nova's eyes. 'There are two big guest houses in the grounds of the Castle itself,' she went on, 'but they haven't many guests just now: the game season is nearly over.'

'I'm *very* glad,' Nova had answered, with a shudder. 'I can't bear to think of wild creatures being hunted.' Her face had looked drawn for a moment and Fiona's eyes had expressed sympathy. She herself, although used to hunting, did not approve of certain types of killing.

'Nor I,' she admitted, 'but we actually see very little of it! It's all well away, over the moors—and I'm assured by the menfolk that, with guns, it's all very quick and merciful.'

The girl's eyes had a suddenly stricken look and Fiona made haste to change the subject.

'Are you looking forward to the party?' she asked brightly. 'Your friend Sara and her parents will be there—and of course, most of the staff and the last few guests, as well as many locals.'

It worked! With a visible effort Nova faced up to the fact that she might often hear the word gun, and talk of killing and must learn to accept it.

The evening had ended cheerfully with the three cousins showing her over the castle, including the portrait gallery. Here, before a great portrait of the present Laird of Glencurran in full highland dress, Nova had stopped with a little gasp, and a strange leap of the heart.

'What's the matter? Do I look so fierce?' His voice had mocked in her ear. She turned slowly, her senses confused, very much aware of his size and strength.

'I don't know! Yes—that is—it—it looked so real for a moment in these soft lights, it rather startled me!'

'Wait until Hallowe'en night,' he uttered laconically and she wondered what he meant.

The next three days flew by as in a dream. After a hectic day of preparation, they were to dine early that evening of October 31st, with Sara, Ian, Fiona and Bruce Robson as guests. Sara's parents were to come later, when the party was under way.

Emerging from her room just before seven, a freshly bathed Nova, looking delightful in a long, full skirted, fine woollen dress of the palest lavender; its narrow edging of pale grey fur framing the low cut neckline; ran lightly along the corridor to the corner.

Here, the great picture gallery was contained in one end of the main corridor; which she now knew also held four big bedrooms, one of which was Glencurran's.

The soft lighting placed at intervals was adequate but Nova was startled beyond all reason as she almost crashed into—the portrait? Come to life? She uttered a little scream as an iron arm caught her close, to prevent her having an undignified tumble.

'Steady! I'm not a ghost, Nova! I told you to wait and see, didn't I?' The brilliant hazel eyes gazed down at the startled, upturned oval of her face. He took in the glossy, blue-black, swinging curls caressing the almost bare white shoulders; the little pearl ear-rings and the matching necklace; even a small pearl and gold clip nestled in the soft fur. The slim hands, pressed against his velvet coat, had pale rose tips.

She saw the flame leap in his eyes, felt the grip tighten round her and instinctively strained away as he bent towards her. At that moment a door opened somewhere in the corridor ahead of them and with an effort, Glencurran controlled himself and releasing her, stepped back, tall and commanding in his wonderful highland regalia.

He took her trembling hand and drew it through his arm, turning towards the great staircase.

'You and I,' he said coolly, 'have got to have a long talk. At the first opportunity—which I shall make!'

Nova gave him a troubled glance; a small smile in response to his, but vouchsafed no reply. In spite of her inner turmoil she enjoyed a wonderful evening, dancing the energetic Scottish way, meeting lots of people, eating too much—and finally falling into bed at two-thirty, completely, but happily, exhausted . . .

When she awoke very late the next day, it

was to find Glencurran had already left for the factory at Fort Augustus, where staff complications had arisen.

It was after ten when she took her tray down the staff stairs to the big kitchen, there to tackle her own washing up. Jane expressed her gratitude briefly.

'We're unco' busy clearing up, y ken,' she smiled, adding eagerly, 'Did ye no' enjoy the party, Miss Helmann?'

Nova laughed, delighted that she could give an honest answer. 'Oh, yes! Mrs Murray, it was wonderful! I haven't enjoyed myself in that way before—ever! We do have Hallowe'en 'do's' in London of course, but somehow I've never been to one. I almost haven't the energy left to walk over to Currabeg, where the Finlays have kindly asked me to coffee. Tomorrow morning I'm off over to the other guest house, and the Alilens.' She turned sparkling eyes to the interested kindly face. 'After lunch Sara is calling to take me to Kinlochieven for tea. I'm going to hate returning to London on Tuesday afternoon—' Nova's eyes grew wistful, 'but I have lots of things to attend to, so go I must! Oh well! If you'll be a dear and just point me in the right direction, I'll be off.' She followed Jane Murray to the back door cheerfully enough.

Jane, hugging her large overall close, stepped out just long enough to point out a gravel path, running away to their left.

'It's aboot five minutes along yon path; still inside the Castle grounds, ye'll no get lost,' she smiled at Nova. 'D'ye think ye would care to ha'e lunch wi' us in the kitchen? It's ay lonely for ye in the dining-room wioot Maister Ross!' She surveyed the girl's face shrewdly.

'What a nice idea! Please, Mrs Murray. Will—we—will Mr Ross be away long, do you know?'

'He left a message to say that he'd phone ye a wee while after lunch,' Jane told her.

Nova walked at a steady pace, inhaling great breaths of the sweet, pine-scented air; glad that her shoes were sturdy and her coat warm, for today was chilly and damp.

The Finlays and their guests were more than pleased to see her and the coffee break was taken in the roomy, but extremely comfortable lounge, before a glowing log fire.

Nova very reluctantly rose to go. Old Colonel Morrell and his sturdy wife had kept her so interested in their tales of the 'good old days', and as the Finlays saw her off, expressing the hope that she would return 'ere long', she knew that her own reluctance to leave this place grew stronger with every passing hour . . .

Glencurran phoned at two-fifteen and Nova found her hands shaking as she took the call.

'Look, Nova,' his deep voice, with its faint Scots accent came to her urgently, 'I want you to cancel your plans for returning to London

102

tomorrow. No—wait—' as he caught her little cry of protest, 'there is something I *must* say to you, and I shall be held up here for a couple of days. I want you to wait for my return. Can ye phone Miss Carstairs and tell her that ye'll be a couple of days later?' The impatience and frustration in his voice gave Nova a sense of panic.

'I *must* get away,' she told herself desperately, 'or perhaps I *never* will! Can't he see that I must prove myself capable of running my own affairs?' She wouldn't, even now, admit to herself that it was her pride; she *wanted* to be restored in *his* eyes. How could she hope for Glencurran's love and respect knowing her weaknesses as he did. Could he really love her in spite of this knowledge? She dare not take the risk!

Glencurran had a shrewd idea of her hidden thoughts and man-like, had decided to tear away the barrier of humiliation which Nova had set up: all his good resolutions forgotten in the urgency of his need to open Nova's eyes to his love.

Her soft voice came to him with equal urgency.

'Oh, Ross! Please,—please understand. I *must* go back now. There are so many ends to tidy up and if I don't go quickly—I—I'll lose my courage again! Don't you see?' She almost sobbed, but controlled it with an effort.

The anguish in her voice moved him deeply,

and he knew that for the moment, he would have to let her go.

His reply came quickly, reassuring her at once. 'All right, little Nova. I do understand, don't worry! I had hoped—well never mind. I shall be in London myself on December the tenth, so I'll see you then. Keep in touch all the time—and *that* is an order! Get Ian to take you to the station and phone the Castle of your safe arrival, see?' He paused long enough for Nova to get her breath—she had been stunned at her apparently easy victory. Colonel Morrell could have told her of the advantage of an orderly retreat, but Nova was happily unaware of the strategy of Glencurran's apparent surrender.

Her relief was so great that she cheerfully agreed to do everything he ordered, and she chatted easily enough for a while longer before he rang off.

She spent a pleasant afternoon and evening with the Ardens, and left with a promise to spend a few days with them in early summer of next year, if not before.

She kept her coffee date with the Allens and left wondering why she felt so at home with all these nice people. Immediately after lunch she bade her farewells to the staff of Castle Glencurran, and set off in the car with Ian, Fiona and Sara.

Her eyes, gazing wistfully at the cold, sparkling waters of the little loch, blurred a little, and as she turned to look back at the castle standing ruggedly on the gentle rise at the head of the loch, with an austere beauty of its own, she told herself with sudden panic, 'I must go—I must—but oh! how I wish I need not!'

Chapter Thirteen

Nova walked briskly, pulling up the collar of her warm suede coat against the chill wind. It was Friday afternoon; she had been back in London for four days.

Her interview with Henry Balfour had been less trying than she had feared: was it possible that she was indeed, now far more capable of facing up to things in general? She had been able to discuss her father's affairs reasonably well, to Balfour's obvious relief, and, he added the news that the price obtained for the town house had been sufficient to cover most of the outstanding debts. Also, they had had an offer of fifty thousand for the small farmhouse in Kent. 'From which, my dear, you should get a fair slice of change,' Balfour assured her.

'I will only take what is left after *all* of Father's commitments are cleared,' she answered firmly. 'I suppose that fifty thousand includes the furnishings and fittings?' she said with shrewdness.

'These last weeks have certainly stiffened the child up,' he thought in silent amazement. Aloud, 'Oh! certainly not, my dear! Though it's quite possible the client would be glad to consider the contents as well. Why don't you run down and check things over? Perhaps your friend Miss Carstairs would go along and give you an idea on values?' He had met Eve Carstairs on several occasions and knew that his young client was in good hands.

Nova considered the idea wistfully now, as she continued on past Kings Road: her preoccupation scarcely allowing her mind to register the busy, jostling assortment of humanity. She did not even notice two of her student friends turn out of Kings Road, but they noticed her, and turned to each other with wide, pleased grins.

'Miss Helmann's back then!' Ricky Phelps muttered bemusedly. His was a dreamy character and he made a habit of stating the obvious. It caused his friends much hilarity.

'Well obviously, fathead!' This from Sue Downy, who considered herself extremely with it, but was in fact more old-fashioned than she realised.

'We'll go along to the shop one day. She was headed that way. Come on!' And she tucked Ricky's arm under her own and led him off.

Nova had by now reached the Chelsea Embankment and here, shortly turned off into the quiet side road wherein Miss Eve Carstairs had the shop that held so many delights.

She stood for a moment, gazing into the well-lit huge bow window. Three other people were also interested in its tasteful display, for in spite of being a little out of the way, it was well known and did remarkably good business.

As the owner seemed to be busy attending

to customers within, Nova continued on to the half-glazed door that, permanently unlocked by day, led to the locked inner door of the flat above the shop. Using her own key, Nova entered another tiny hall, to the right of which, was a second door leading into the shop, then ran lightly up the dim staircase and along to her bedroom.

By the time Eve had finished serving her customers, Nova had prepared a light tea of thin ham sandwiches and small tea cakes. She looked up with a rosy face as her mother's old friend plumped down in one of the two fireside chairs.

'Have you started an early seasonal rush?' she queried with a laugh, placing the tray within easy reach of her friend's elbow.

'Well, it's only seven weeks, dear child! Always a good idea to get in a few things early,' Eve replied calmly. She paused to take an appreciative sip of tea. 'Um! I wanted this! Do you know, I've just sold that lovely Spode teapot! To a young dentist, for his wife! I think she must be a fairly new wife, because he said 'she's worth every penny of it' and paid—in cash—without a tremor!' Her eyes twinkled as they met Nova's.

How good it was to see the child looking well again; the convalescence in Scotland must have worked wonders. The girl seemed much more self-reliant too; with a determination in her every word and action. Only once or twice had Eve Carstairs caught a slightly puzzled look in the violet-blue eyes. These had been the unguarded moments when Nova had found herself waiting with impatient eagerness, for mail from Scotland.

Obedient to Glencurran's wishes, she had phoned the Castle of her safe arrival, to be told that 'Mr Ross will phone ye, he ses, as soon as he gets back'. Ross had not phoned as yet and Nova was indeed annoyed with herself for feeling such disappointment.

After dinner that evening, with herself and Nova snugly settled before a cheerful fire, Eve Carstairs begged her young friend to take on a full time job, helping her run the shop.

'You do know a little about antiques, dear, and I'd be so glad of your help with the bookwork, and of course—' with a sudden shrewd glance at the quiet face opposite, 'you can leave me with only a minimum of notice, anytime you like!'

Nova turned misty eyes on her hostess's kind, thin face. 'Dear Miss Carstairs! How very sweet you have been to me. It is the kind of work I like, and of course I'd like to do it full time—but—I must get a flat of my own soon. I just can't take over your spare room indefinitely!'

'But Nova! Of course you can! If you are going to settle here in town, for a time at any rate, where better?' She raised fine brows quizzically.

'W-ell! If you are certain I won't be a pest—then I should like to stay. It's going to take a few months to settle all my father's affairs—and with a friend to unburden myself to now and then, I shall cope better for being settled.' She proceeded to bring Eve up to date on her interview with Henry Balfour, ending with his suggestion that they go down to Kent and value the contents of the house.

'If you are not in any desperate hurry, my dear, I'd love to come with you! What about the first Sunday after Christmas? Weather permitting, we could motor down? Or otherwise go by—' At that moment the loud peal of the phone made them both jump.

Nova's face paled and then flushed rosily.

You answer it dear, your legs are younger than mine!' But a thoughtful smile played about the wide mouth as she watched the girl rise quickly and go to the little antique table, just outside the lounge door. She leaned back to close her eyes, relaxing, as the slightly breathless tones of the girl's voice came to her faintly, from beyond the half-closed door.

Nova had taken a deep, deep breath before taking up the receiver. 'Is that Miss Helmann? Good! Nova, Ross here.' As if she'd needed to be told! 'I'm sorry not to have phoned you before this, but I stayed on after the trouble was cleared to attend some business of my own. Now! How are things with you?'

Nova cleared her throat nervously and told

him briefly, that all was well, and that she was to start work as Miss Carstairs' full time assistant, as from Monday.

'I see! Determined to establish independence, eh? Well, I've no doubt it'll do fine for the time being, but ye ken, my wee lassie, that I've a few ideas of my own for ye?'—broadening his accent deliberately to keep things on a light note.

'It's a job I like, and it will do *very* well indeed, thank you,' she answered, with a breathless laugh, adding, 'I don't *need* any other ideas, I have plenty of my own!'

'We'll see!' he uttered laconically then diplomatically changed the subject. 'I'll be in London for a few days, from December the tenth as I told you, and I want you to keep at least two evenings free for me! I understand from Sara that it's your birthday on the twelfth of November? I just wish we could get together for it! Never mind, I'll make it up to you when we meet.' There was unmistakable laughter in the deep voice.

'Oh, no! Really, you don't have to Ross— but—' she gave a breathless little chuckle, surprised at the truth of her own next words, 'I *will* be pleased to save those evenings for you.'

She sounded so sincere that his heart sang. A few more exchanges and then he was gone, leaving Nova strangely bereft but happily anticipating the coming meetings. After all, he was such *good* company—when he wasn't browbeating her, she excused herself, in confusion . . .

For some moments she remained standing by the little table, conjuring up incidents from the strangely unreal time on Curransay. How remote it all seemed now and yet it was also just at the back of her conscious mind, no matter how resolutely she forced herself not to think of it! Always, it came back to the humiliation she felt in the face of her weakness before Glencurran. How hard it was going to be to restore her pride to her own satisfaction . . .

She sighed deeply, and then stooped to lift Sulah, Miss Carstair's Siamese cat, close in her arms.

'Come on Su-Su, let's go and get you some milk and attend to supper for your mistress,' and she peeped into the silent lounge, to retreat, smiling quietly, as she saw her friend's relaxed features.

She prepared a tray with hot chocolate and buttered savoury biscuits while Sulah drank his milk, then laughed as he trotted ahead of her into the lounge, with great dignity, his deep-throated 'miaow' rousing Eve from her doze.

'Was that your friend from Scotland, dear?' she enquired gently.

'Yes! He is coming to London in December. The tenth, he said. I am to spend a couple of evenings with him then.' She coloured faintly. 'I would so like you to meet him, Miss

112

Carstairs. May I arrange for him to call here?'

Eve replaced her cup and saucer, smiling her delight. 'Why certainly, Nova! This is your home for the time being, and being such an old friend anyway, of course I should love to meet any more recent friends of yours!' Her kind, light blue gaze rested keenly on the slight flush still evident on the girl's smooth cheeks.

'You met Mr Glencurran through dear old Lossie, I believe you said?' she continued quietly.

'That's right! Sara and her people knew his family very well too. He—he was very kind to me whilst I was at—at Lossie's place—but—he has this idea that I n-need looking after all the time!' She raised her eyes to meet Eve's, a peculiar expression in their depths. 'Complete nonsense, or course, so I—I'll be glad to let him see that I have staunch friends, who *know* that I am quite capable.'

Eve found something quite pathetic about Nova's dissertation. The child had certainly appeared to have been lively and self-reliant enough on the surface of things, but hadn't her illness been proof enough that she was virtually *insecure*? Eve had known the family for years. She was well aware that Nova had felt unwanted by her father and this, coupled with the terrible physical shock of finding his body, would surely have broken the nerve of many a stronger character?

'So what,' she asked herself, 'was this man

113

trying to do to her old friend's daughter? Make her lean on him? Or possibly goad her into standing firmly on her own two feet? Yes! That was it she felt sure! Hadn't Nova returned from Scotland with a new air of resolution? And wasn't she, in spite of liking this man, too ready to defend her independence against him?' Eve felt sure that she had summed up the situation well, and felt herself eager to meet Glencurran and to judge what kind of 'friend' Nova had acquired!

Chapter Fourteen

On Monday morning an eager and willing Nova began her full time work for her old friend. She was, of course, completely familiar with the shop's lay out but Eve had added quite a few small, but very good pieces to her stock. One whole corner of the large front room was tastefully arranged with a varied and delightful display of small *objets d'art*. These included vinaigrettes, snuff boxes, porcelain figurines, a good selection of heavy Victorian jewellery, and small paintings.

'I'd be glad to have you take over this section for me Nova! I'll be on hand to help and advise in your busier moments—of which I'm sure there will be plenty!'

They smiled at each other quietly and Eve went off to select a piece from her store-room with which to refill the gap left by the sale of a small Regency bureau she had sold recently.

Left to herself, Nova settled down to study and check the articles in her charge against a neatly-typed list Eve had given her.

Her first customer pounced with delight on two genuine 'boneshaker' fairings which, she declared, would complete a set of six, for her husband, an ardent collector of these pert, colourful Victorian, cycling figurines.

A little later she diligently helped a *very*

elderly gentleman search for a vinaigrette. 'As near as possible to one my wife had as a girl, given her by her mother on her sixteenth birthday, y' know!'

His faded old eyes had twinkled at the sweet-faced girl, so obviously sincere in her desire to help.

'What a lovely idea, sir! I do hope we can find one—oh! you have a little sketch. That should be very helpful!' And she took it from the thin, slightly tremulous old hand.

'What a way she has,' Eve thought as she came back to supervise the placing of the new piece. For a brief moment she watched the two heads close together over the little trinkets; the silvery-white one, leaning stiffly from the chair before the counter; the girl's, glossy, thick, with little blue lights snapping as it caught the bright glow from well-placed wall lights.

She turned away with a smile as Nova gave a pleased exclamation.

'Ah! here it is, sir, almost identical to the little drawing!' She held up a little, silver box; the lid lavishly designed with acanthus, a large amethyst set in the centre bloom. It opened to show the gilded inside and the little grille whose purpose was to retain the fragment of acid or perfume soaked sponge: the deodoriser of long ago.

Nova wondered fleetingly, how many dainty ladies had cleverly added perfume to the little sponge . . . probably most of them! She had been so interested in her customer's story, brief though it was. The original gift had been made to his wife long after the vinaigrette had gone out of fashion. How had it left her possession and could the one purchased by her husband today be the same one?

She woke from her reverie, startled, as Eve's voice came, 'Lunch-time, my dear! Let's lock up and go aloft.'

They used the living-room-kitchen behind the shop for coffee break and afternoon tea, but Eve liked lunch in the flat. It was always left prepared by the pleasant woman who had been Eve's daily for years, so all they had to do was finish it off and eat it!

Over the weekend they had arranged very satisfactory terms, and Nova considered herself very lucky indeed. She said so again now.

'Nonsense, dear child! It's to our mutual benefit. Don't you think that Mrs Prowse and Burnes were pleased that you are staying on with me?'

Yesterday afternoon they had driven in Eve's new Avenger to the house off Draycott Avenue, to settle the last few details. Nova had felt a hollow in the pit of her stomach, but once inside her old home, the warmth of welcome from her old staff had so moved her, that she had found herself in the position of cheering *them* up!

Over a cup of tea in the staff sitting-room, they had assured her that all her wishes had been taken care of; the pieces chosen for her own eventual flat, sent off to store; the one or two items she had given them as gifts from her own possessions carefully removed and the new owners well satisfied to retain their services until 'moving in' time when they would then move out. Only Milly was to stay; she would help to select a new staff. Mrs Prowse and Mr Burnes were to retire.

She agreed with Eve's cheerful remark now. 'Oh, they were! Bless them, they really have been worried about me! It's nice to know that our visit eased their minds.' She gave a misty smile and began clearing the dishes.

Eve rose to do her share, following her into the kitchen. 'Nova, dear, I rather want to accept an invite to dinner for both of us—on Tuesday—how will you feel about it?'

The girl turned a thoughtful face towards the older woman as she ran the hot water. 'In a public place you mean, Miss Carstairs? All right—I think! It will be a nice change for us both, eh!' Her sweet smile was only a little cautious.

'I meant particularly—how would it affect you to bump into Steven Blanchard?' Eve qualified.

Nova took a deep breath, then began briskly, but carefully, to wash the dishes. 'Oh! not too badly, I think! At first it was an awful hurt; then I grew angry; now—I feel very slightly contemptuous. I should behave in quite a civilised manner though! No dramatic scenes; just polite indifference.'

Eve Carstairs felt an immense relief, and bestowed a light kiss on the soft, young cheek.

'Well done, dear! It *was* a contemptible thing to do, especially as gossip has it—his own slate isn't too clean!' She made a rueful mouth and rather wished she'd not uttered the last remark.

'Oh?' Nova's finely-arched brows expressed surprise, but she didn't press the point. 'Well, it really is a matter of complete indifference to me now, dear.' She took a quick look at her wrist-watch. 'Ah, me! Lunch-hour's over, let's get busy again.'

'Busy again' set the pattern of the following days. They went to tea with an old friend of Eve's on Sunday; mid-morning on Monday, Henry Balfour phoned to say that the Kent property sale had been completed, including contents at later valuation, and that all being well she might be able to keep at least half of the proceeds. Then just before closing time on Tuesday, Nova renewed her friendship with Ricky Phelps and Sue Downy, and the taking up of old threads gave Nova genuine pleasure.

With every passing day, she felt her confidence at meeting the people she had known before her father's death, increasing. She also found herself really looking forward to the dinner date arranged by Eve for that evening.

They were to be called for by their hosts and were ready on the dot, as the private doorbell pealed musically through the flat.

Eve introduced her business friends to her young assistant, then turned to the smiling girl. 'Nova, my dear, say hello to Ivor and Leila Dinsdale.'

Nova was made to feel instantly relaxed by the mature charm and kindliness of the Dinsdales, an elderly, childless couple; who had known Eve Carstairs for over twelve years.

During a very pleasant evening Nova was delighted to learn that they had assisted her mother to find two or three good paintings for the house in Kent. She questioned them eagerly on their acquaintance with 'Mimsey'.

'I remember her very well,' Ivor assured her. 'She had a particular love of Hogarth's "family" paintings.'

'They are still there,' Nova told him quietly. 'We spent a few weeks of each year there when I was a little girl. Somehow tho', I don't seem to have been able to get down this last eighteen months or so.'

As they were leaving, a very familiar voice spoke almost in her ear. 'Why, Nova! What a surprise meeting you here! I thought—that is—friends told me that you were staying in Scotland!' The man who had spoken, had the grace to colour, briefly, as his almost black eyes met the cool, violet-blue gaze turned up to his face.

'Hello, Steven. I *have* been staying with some *very* good friends in Invernsshire, yes! but I have been back for almost two weeks.'

He hadn't missed the emphasis, but ignoring it, said smoothly, 'It's good to see you looking so much better. As a matter of fact, you look delightful.' A sudden flash in the lovely eyes caused him to add, hastily, 'Look here, my dear, we can't talk here, can we? There is no reason why we shouldn't keep in touch—for old times' sake y'know! How about lunching with me, let's say on Friday? At the Riverside, eh?' He waited confidently for her acceptance, trusting to his knowledge of her innate courtesy.

His smooth, patronising manner set Nova's teeth on edge. She wondered suddenly, how could she have consented to marry this smug, self-opinionated person. Aloud, she said indifferently, 'A very good idea. There is something I wish to hand over to you—personally! Pick me up at one o'clock sharp, please. I have only an hour for lunch.' And she coolly turned on her heel and re-joined her waiting friends, answering Eve's troubled look with a warm hand squeeze—filling that kindly person with heartfelt relief . . .

The man stood for a long moment, following the girl's glowing figure with angry eyes; then his expression changed to one of calculation. Little Nova had changed! She hadn't shown that kind of spirit before, or that charming self-assurance! It might be worth his while, he thought now, to get closer to her on a different basis. Surely under her present circumstances and in view of the scandal attached to her father's death, she would be fair game?

For Steven Blanchard, son of a very good family and on the surface so highly respectable, was by no means above reproach in his personal dealings with women.

Chapter Fifteen

Nova woke reluctantly, to a chilly November morning, and lay for several moments, pondering the sense of importance that invaded her mind. Then she remembered! It was her twenty-fourth birthday—and her father would not share it!

Her eyes filled as she recalled the happiness of birthdays when her mother was alive; the way she had insisted that Charles should make a point of having tea with his wife and little daughter whenever the demands of business allowed.

He had always agreed, and indeed, had obviously enjoyed these birthday attentions to his only child, but after her mother's death, apart from his always generous gifts, he had given her no personal attention at all on her birthdays. In fact he was often away at the time, leaving her gift with Lossie and later with Mrs Prowse.

Nova indulged her moment of sadness and then made a valiant effort to put it to the back of her mind. At the breakfast-table she greeted Eve with a cheerful smile. Her face lit up with surprised delight when Eve leaned down to place a pile of mail by her plate.

'Happy birthday, my dear,' she said, bestowing a light kiss on the upturned face.

'Thank you, Miss Carstairs. I c-can see I shall be slow with my breakfast this m-morning,' Nova said, blinking rapidly. She honestly hadn't expected so many people to remember!

There were cards from Sara, Mr and Mrs Arden, from Miss Lossiemuir, from Mrs Prowse, Mr Burnes and Milly. Also, and these were a great surprise, from Fiona and Ian, the staff at Castle Glencurran and the Grahams from Oban. Closer to home again, one from Eve and also Ricky and Sue.

She came at last to a large registered envelope, with a flat oblong hump in its thick centre, and with slightly shaky hands, she turned it over to read the sender's address. It was from Ross Glencurran!

It seemed to take ages to open, but at last she drew forth a large card and a small, jeweller's box. She gently opened the lid to give a gasp of mingled dismay and delight.

Twinkling up at her innocently was a large silver brooch, its centre-piece a perfectly designed thistle, set with amethyst and tiny diamonds. It was exquisite.

'I-I can't accept this . . . can I?' Nova turned appealing eyes to her friend and employer.

'Certainly you can . . . and drink your coffee, it's almost cold,' Eve answered calmly. 'Why don't you read the card, my dear?'

A bemused Nova did so. It was a very nice one, slightly formal, but with a handwritten message begging her to wear the gift when she kept their dinner date, and to have a very good day, and not to forget him?

It was such a casually affectionate message, that Nova gave a breathless little laugh and touched the lovely brooch with a tentative finger. 'He can be rather sweet,' she told herself, 'and not really possible to forget.'

Which was precisely the reaction Ross had hoped for. He would have been even more delighted had he known that Nova was finding it more difficult to forget him with every passing day.

Just before four-thirty, a florist's van drew up outside the shop and Nova, who was in the middle of packing a delicate Dresden figurine, saw Eve take a large spray from the delivery man.

They entered the shop living-room a few moments later and Eve motioned to the spray lying on the small oaken table.

'There's a card attached, my dear. You go ahead while I make us a quick cuppa.'

The flowers, great shaggy chrysanthemums, were lovely; spicy and fresh, and Nova buried her face in them before reading the card. They were from Miles Tremayne; a further warm wish and the added statement that he would see them both later on that evening.

'What are you planning, Miss Carstairs, dear?' she queried.

'Just Mr Tremayne to dinner and one or two

friends after. We must have a modest 'do', mustn't we?'

It developed into a very pleasant evening indeed; the one or two friends turned out to be the Dinsdales, and to Nova's delight, the married daughter and her husband, of her old neighbours whom she remembered, had sent a warmly sympathetic note of condolence all those long months ago. She felt a moment of shame, when she remembered that she had neither acknowledged the letter, nor called in on her recent visit to her old home.

Her stammered apology was cut short gently by Peggy Blaine, who kissed her warmly and pushed a huge box of chocolates into her arms.

'It's wonderful to see you looking so well,' she uttered.

The pleasant memory of the evening still lingered as she sped lightly down to the shop the following day. The morning sped busily away and she had completely forgotten her luncheon date with Blanchard. She was reminded of it by Sue and Ricky who came in with two fellow students to browse around—as usual! They hadn't yet, to her knowledge, ever purchased anything, but Eve was surprisingly tolerant of these investigations of her varied stock.

Today however, Ricky surprised Nova by asking her to choose and put by for him, one from among several heavy Victorian necklaces. 'Something that you think will suit Sue's looks and colouring,' he hissed, with a furtive glance at the other three. 'Take this as a deposit and I'll slip in next week on my own,' and he slid three pound coins across to an amused but co-operative Nova.

It was now twelve forty-five and Sue ambled up to say, 'How about us treating you to a burger, Miss Helmann?'—and it was then she remembered her date with Steven Blanchard.

'I am sorry, dears! May we make it one day next week? Oh good, and thank you for that nice card. Bye-bye.'

She hurried over to Eve as they left and explained about the forgotten date with Blanchard. 'I had forgotten it completely. May I rush off now? Oh, bless you—thanks.' And she sped away to freshen up, running downstairs in time to walk calmly through the shop door as Blanchard, in a racy M.G. drew into the kerb.

After exchanging a cool greeting, Nova sat in silence until Blanchard pulled into a parking place in Queen Street Place, and moments later he pushed open the entrance door of Riverside and waited with a slightly strained smile for Nova to precede him.

She was looking, he mused, damned attractive in a rust-coloured suede coat. The head waiter hurried forward and showed them to a table near the window. As they were served pleasantly and efficiently with an excellent lunch, Steven Blanchard began to compliment her smoothly on her appearance, letting his eyes wander deliberately to the creamy throat and rounded bosom, revealed now by a dress of soft woollen material in pale green. Nova raised cold, indifferent eyes to his.

'You never used to pay me any compliments, Steven! Am I really any different?'

'I must have been blind, my dear! You seem to have acquired more self-possession—and dare I say—fire!' He gave her a confident smile, feeling sure that it would awaken some response born of the memories of their short and lukewarm engagement—but . . . Nova had only contempt for this man.

She realised how unaroused she had been. She knew the real thing now but must prove herself worthy.

'I don't think I look any better than before,' she told him with an edge to the soft voice.

'Oh, but you do! More . . . more responsive, more glowing! Nova! We really must keep in touch my dear. Surely we have known each other long enough for that?' His smile was charming, but it left the recipient unmoved.

'I don't think we *knew* each other at all,' said the new Nova, adding briskly, 'I *do* only have an hour for lunch—so . . . !'

He took the hint, and it was only after twenty minutes of steady eating and casual chat that Nova came to the point of her keeping this date at all. Certainly, she had no intention of encouraging Blanchard's illusions.

She moved her coffee cup to one side and slid a small package across to Blanchard's side of the table. 'I'm sorry not to have returned it before—but I was—rather busy,' she stated casually. She might have been returning a borrowed book, so indifferent did she feel about handing back the lovely square-cut emerald and diamond ring.

Her eyes met his steadily, and again he felt at a disadvantage, as he palmed the little package and slid it quickly into his coat pocket. He answered her look with a somewhat strained smile, but said merely, 'Thank you, Nova. It has been pleasant, I hope you will come again? May I phone you?' He kept his eyes lowered as he asked the question, reluctant to betray his anger and chagrin. He could wait . . . and hope!

'Thank *you*, Steven. I always enjoy coming here. No, I don't think there would be any point in our meeting again like this, do you? We may bump into each other round and about, of course! Now, I must fly.' Nova rose with the grace Blanchard remembered.

They had gone through the doors by now and she turned away from him with a brief wave of the small gloved hand. 'Goodbye— and thank you again for lunch.' She had refused a lift back.

Blanchard watched her go, with a smouldering fury mounting in his narrowed eyes; then turning up his overcoat collar against the cold wind blowing across the icy waters of the Thames, he walked jerkily away towards his parked car.

Nova entered the shop puffing; her glowing face and pink nose bringing a smile to Eve's face. 'Oh dear! Three minutes late—be with you in a moment.' She hurried through to the back, here to shed her outdoor garments and to emerge again in the lovely green woollen dress given her by Eve yesterday.

'Well that's that,' she uttered composedly. 'Mr Steven Blanchard now has his ring back— and I honestly pity the next poor girl to get it!'

A delighted Eve could hardly believe the evidence of her own ears. Little Nova was certainly standing on her own two feet.

Chapter Sixteen

The weekend passed quickly to a Nova rapidly filling a mind that had been closed and empty for so long, with so many and varied things of interest, that she wondered if life couldn't become too hectic! She did make time on Sunday afternoon to answer all her birthday mail with thank you letters; three of which became so long, she finally complained of an aching elbow and hand.

'I really do have writer's cramp—and it's horrid!' she complained.

Eve, getting ready to go out to tea with a friend, laughed. 'You must be finding plenty to write about,' she teased.

'To dear old Lossie and Sara—yes! But I'm a bit foxed about Ross's.' Nova tried to keep her tone deceptively casual.

'I wouldn't have thought so!' Eve stated somewhat drily. 'Three whole pages to say thank you for that lovely brooch?'

'I—er—haven't mentioned it yet,' sheepishly. 'I've been so busy telling him of all the things that keep me so busy and er—contented.'

'Hm! Well, don't forget to ask him to make time for tea with us, or perhaps an evening—when he visits London, will you? Bye for now, be back by seven,' and Eve left, smiling to herself.

Later, Nova played records, finding among Eve's varied collection, an L.P. by one Jamie Phillips; whose romantic Scots tenor reminded her vividly of the Hallowe'en party at Glencurran Castle.

For a moment her mind conjured up a startling picture of Glencurran as he had looked that night; tall, dominating and rugged in his beautiful highland costume. She gave herself an angry little shake and deliberately forced herself to think of his brutality on the island, and of her own overwhelming sense of shame and humiliation. It did not quite work! The hatred she had felt she should maintain was already fading, to be replaced by a great longing for his physical presence.

Nova shook a bewildered head. Why, now that they were separated by hundreds of miles, did she feel herself so increasingly aware of him? Her mind recalled his sheer masculine strength so vividly that she gave a great shudder and threw a nervous look over her shoulder. 'Idiot!' she chided herself tersely, and hastily rejected the lovely recording for one of noisy and tempestuous beat; not really her taste, but leaving one little time for recalling things better forgotten. But those things persisted in her innermost thoughts . . . and she was almost glad.

During the following week, Nova had lunch with Ricky, Sue and a Jamaican girl who was introduced to her as Emerald. 'Emmy for short,' Sue laughed, 'She's studying economics, but she's always broke—aren't you, Emmy?' The good-natured laughter that followed augmented a relaxed and friendy atmosphere, and when they parted the three girls had made firm plans to meet on Saturday to share a Christmas shopping jaunt in the always exciting West End.

Later in the week Ricky managed to sneak into the shop without Sue, and with Nova's help, settled for a lovely old silver and topaz necklace which Nova declared to be exactly 'Sue'.

'Yeah!' Ricky agreed laconically. 'Matches her eyes!'

The three girls spent a happy, but exhausting Saturday morning in and around Oxford Street, and were glad to find seats at a table in Sue and Emmy's favourite coffee bar in the Kings Road on their return to their own area. They sank down gratefully, depositing packages around them.

Nova flexed sore fingers and looked up to meet the amused face of Steven Blanchard. His deep set eyes glanced casually at the other two girls, before addressing himself to Nova. 'Hello again, my dear! May I join you for a few moments?' And at her reluctant permission, he seated himself. Nova raised coolly questioning eyebrows at him, determined not to be too forthcoming beyond casual good manners.

'I understand from a friend that you are flat hunting?' he murmured, and at her brief, 'I was, not now though,' he added, 'Oh! pity! I have actually written you about one, as I—er—certainly didn't expect to bump into you again so soon, but under the circs it won't interest you, eh?' He smiled at her easily, but a little flame of frustration lit the back of his cold eyes, not unnoticed by the watchful eyes of Nova's friends.

He had hoped to use the promised flat as a point of contact with Nova over a period of weeks. Her brief statement had temporarily floored him.

Nova felt herself to have been a little bad mannered. 'Thank you, just the same, Steven. Perhaps if I need it later, I might get in touch about it?'

'Well . . . the friend isn't moving until two days before Christmas, but I guess he will have let it go by then!' he replied smoothly.

He stayed for a moment longer, hurrying off with a warm smile at Nova, and a casual nod at her companions who seemed to have met him before? She queried this as soon as he got beyond hearing.

'Oh, yes!' Emmy said drily, 'we've met him on one or two occasions, haven't we, Sue? Mostly at parties!' She gave a lopsided smile at Nova's raised eyebrows. 'Oh, he wears shaded glasses and a wig; he looks like one of the 'in' set then, y'see! But it isn't *generally* known that

134

he and one or two of his friends have been to quite a few slightly questionable gatherings. Those types are—er—considered to be so . . . elite? and respectable—aren't they?'

'Nova! I'm sorry, we shouldn't be talking like this,' Sue began remorsefully, remembering the broken engagement.

'Nonsense. I'm just *very* surprised, that's all! I thought he had such concern for his reputation? I realise now that it was adverse publicity he feared!'

There was a faint bitterness in the soft voice which both girls noted. They made haste to change the conversation, and on a more carefree note, they parted company having planned to meet again at a party to which Sue and Emmy had been invited.

'A respectable one, I hope?' Nova queried half jokingly.

Sue regarded her seriously. 'Well—they seem to start that way, Nova. Some—not *all*—mind you—seem to take a turn for the worse towards one or two o'clock! These are the ones we leave early! In fact—I believe this was how we offended Mr Blanchard! He had—er—certain ideas for entertaining his friends after the party and Emmy and I snubbed him and left.'

'Thanks for the warning, Sue! If he turns up at this one, we'll all leave early, eh?' Nova realised suddenly how lucky was her escape.

'Sure! Ricky *insists* on it.' They waved once

as they crossed the road and Nova, feeling somewhat shattered at their revelations hurried back to the shop.

They were so busy during the following days, that the party almost slipped her mind. During the last weekend of November, Eve made up her mind to close the shop for the entire week after Christmas; suggesting, to Nova's delight, that they spend it at a small hotel in Kent and take their time sorting out the contents of the little farmhouse on the outskirts of Meopham.

'Lovely! Eve dear.' She had shyly submitted to pressure about using her old friend's Christian name. 'I can improve on that. We have a very nice woman who has kept it clean for us for years. I'll get in touch right away and then we can stay there. The new owner will not mind, he doesn't move in until February.'

'Splendid! Nova, is the farmhouse your favourite? More so than the town house I mean?'

'Oh yes! I've always loved it. It was Mimsey's too, I think! It was *really* lovely there! So peaceful and yet so much fun. We went there for several Christmases running, I remember. From when I was about five, until the year before Mimsey d-died. Dad used to join us on the morning of Christmas Eve and we *really* all seemed so close at those times.'

'No summer holidays there, dear?'

'Oh, lots! Yes! On several occasions I went

136

alone with Lossie, while Dad took Mimsey on short cruises and continental holidays. But I'm sure she liked it best when we three were at Brambledene. I know she'd always planned to transfer some of her favourite pieces from town to Kent, although Brambledene was delightfully furnished.'

Eve was about to ask another sympathetic question when the midday post came.

'Two for you, dear. Save 'em for lunch break?' And as Nova at that moment got an eager American customer, of whom they had many, she could only nod cheerful agreement.

By the time the American was gone, it was time for lunch and they hurried up to the warm brightness of the flat; seeming the more cheerful by contrast with the chilly November drizzle which persisted outside.

'Horrid, isn't it?' Nova said as they settled before the fire, adding compulsively, 'It has been snowing in northern Scotland you know!'

Eve's eyes twinkled. 'So the papers inform one! Let's be rude dear, and eat and read.'

Nova's first one was from Sara; writing to say that she and a friend were coming to stay with Uncle Miles for Christmas, and that he was then returning to Scotland with them for a week, taking in Hogmanay. 'We shall see each other, Nova dear,' she went on, 'because I know Uncle plans for us all to get together over Christmas.'

Nova hadn't been especially looking

forward to the holiday, but now she felt her spirits rise. The second letter was from Glencurran; his last, he stated, before the coming trip to London. 'I shall ring you the moment I reach my hotel,' he went on, 'that will be around six-thirty in the evening, so stay handy.' Nova could hear the command in his voice so clearly that she looked up with startled eyes, surprised that Eve seemed unaware of it. She read on, 'I have also booked three evenings for us, out of the seven I shall be there, Nova, and I hope that Miss Carstairs will honour me by joining us on the second or third of these? I have already written to her on the matter and I hope she won't say no! 'She wouldn't dare!' Nova thought caustically.

She folded the letter thoughtfully and wondered why his two or three letters had left her with an urge to stamp her foot and yell. She always started reading them with a nervous tremor, which ended in high indignation at his unmistakable air of masculine patronage. 'He can't treat me as tho' I were a stupid little girl one moment and a desirable woman the next,' she told herself stormily. But he does! the inner voice mocked and she bounced up, startling an absorbed Eve, to start clearing the lunchtable with unnecessary clatter.

Later, they discussed dates and Eve found herself quite free to accept Glencurran's 'kind invitation'. Nova met her twinkling eyes and found herself laughing helplessly. She controlled herself with difficulty, shaking her glossy, blue-black curls.

'He's—he's so . . .' she began.

'Bossy?' Eve suggested smoothly. Nova could only nod agreement, the laughter, good to hear, bubbling up again.

She was only reminded of the party she was to attend when Sue and Ricky came into the shop on the Tuesday before.

Sue was hoping to get hold of a piece of scrimshaw, 'For me Dad,' she told Eve.

She took about twenty minutes to make her choice from their rather limited collection, and only then threw a casual reminder over her shoulder as she and Ricky left.

'Don't be late on Saturday, Nova! We'll pick you up at eight sharp in Tod's ol' banger.'

Nova raised her hand in acknowledgement of the reminder and smiled at their disappearing backs. She hadn't missed the special look in the 'topaz' coloured eyes as they met Ricky's now and then; or the way his hand had grasped Sue's when they left.

'I wonder!' she murmured to herself.

Chapter Seventeen

'Nova darling! Are you sure that you'll be all right alone here until tomorrow afternoon?' Eve had asked the question anxiously at least three times during the last couple of hours and Nova, ready for the party, turned to reassure her.

'*Perfectly* safe, not in the *least* nervous, and I'll be *extra* careful about locking all doors and windows to the flat—there! You enjoy your overnight stay with Mrs Knight and we'll have lots to talk over tomorrow evening.'

'All right, pet! The alarm system is set; the local police will do their usual kind patrol when I'm away—that should be a comfort, eh?' Nova nodded cheerful agreement. 'And you intend leaving the party before midnight anyway, so I shall leave the hall and staircase lights on and the outer door unlocked, dear,' Eve stated firmly.

'That will be nice! It's a bit spooky coming in to complete darkness and if Sulah runs down to meet me I shan't trip over him! Are you all ready Eve, or can I give you a hand?'

'No, thank you, my dear. I'm ready now, but I shan't leave until nine o'clock. It's only an hour's run from here. Oh! is that your friends?' as a sharp blast on a car horn sounded outside.

It was and Nova sped off to join them in the most disreputable old car she had ever seen.

'However did it pass its MOT?' she queried.

'It's only got four months to go—and it won't pass another!' its owner informed her resignedly. He threw her a cheeky grin over his shoulder as, with a grinding of gears, the 'banger' juddered into motion.

Sue hastily introduced Nova to Tod, a thin intense type, adding that Emmy and her friend Geoff had declined a lift and were going ahead on foot.

'I'm not surprised!' Nova stated frankly, and they all laughed, Tod stopping long enough to warn her that he'd make her walk too, if she got too personal about his car.

They arrived at the shabby old house in Clapham Road, where the party was being held, to find Emmy and Geoff, a tall, good looking Jamaican, waiting in the front porch for them. After cheerful exchanges, they were hustled in with one or two other arrivals. The heat of the rather bare hall hit them like a solid wall after the sharp coldness outside.

Her host—whose name she never learned—plied her with food and drink, grabbed a small, curly haired brunette, and pushed his way to the middle of an already crowded room where they went through the motions known as 'dancing' today.

'That's his wife, Barry,' Emmy said in her ear, as she wriggled by with Geoff, both doing

141

their own version of the same dance while managing to look in complete rhythmic agreement.

Two hours later, Nova had developed a mild headache and was more than glad to sit out with Ricky and Sue.

'Did you know that Steven Blanchard came in about half an hour ago?' Sue asked, plopping on to a cushion beside Nova.

Ricky had found one of the few chairs and he placed it so that Sue could lean back against his knees.

'No! I hadn't noticed him. Where? Oh, yes! he has just caught my eye.' She smiled and raised a casual hand at the head just seen above a close knot of people wedged in the big bay window area.

Sue and Ricky exchanged quick glances and then Sue, with a flush staining her usually pale cheeks, turned anxiously to the other girl.

'As a matter of fact—we—that is—er—Ricky and I, were wondering if you'd do us a *very* great f-favour?' She met Nova's surprised eyes bravely. 'Rick and I are goin' to be married on New Year's Day. We had intended sharing his bedsit after—! It's awful cheek, we know, 'specially since you and he—well,' she hesitated, then rushed on eagerly, 'do you think you could ask him to put you in touch with that man who had the flat to let, Nova?' Her wide, anxious eyes gazed hopefully into Nova's.

'What great news! I'm honestly delighted for you both! About the other—well, I don't know, dears! Couldn't you *both* approach him?' She raised a rather puzzled look at Ricky.

'He wouldn't entertain us at all!' he jerked out. 'We—er—had a few words with him some time ago and he doesn't forget—or forgive! It's just the owner's name and address we'd like. We could take it from there—if it isn't already too late.' The despondency in his usually placid voice smote Nova's heart. It *was* so difficult for young people to find places these days and it took a great deal of very real courage to stand by the conventions and to find and establish the perfect freedom of one's own home.

Tod came back just then with a drink, and she seized the moment to raise her glass, wishing them happiness and luck.

'Don't worry, old beans! I'll have a chat to Steve, and if he can't help, I'll ask around other people!'

During the next hour she managed to exchange a few words with Blanchard, and even shared a dance with him. The party got noisier and hotter and as their dance ended, he pressed for another but she shook her head firmly, setting the blue-black curls dancing.

'Thank you, Steven, but I've had enough. It's home for me right now!' She threw him a smile and made to move off in search of Sue to tell her that she was leaving, but he retained her elbow.

'Wait, Nova! Please let me run you back to the shop. I can return here after. It'll go on until tomorrow morning and it's only,' with a quick glance at his wrist watch, 'eleven-thirty.' He gave her a hopeful smile, meant to be flattering but Nova wasn't moved by it, and was about to refuse when she thought of Sue and Ricky's plea. Perhaps this short run would give her the opportunity to discuss the flat? She could but try and it wasn't very far. It would be strictly business. She accepted a cigarette whilst he had a quick word with their hosts, but had stubbed it out after a short while and finding no handy ash tray she put it into her small bag.

Fifteen minutes later, his car turned back across Chelsea Bridge, above a river sparkling like black ice, and a few moments later drew up outside the shop. Blanchard climbed out and walked round to help Nova out into the road, quiet and empty but for a dark car parked several yards further up. He walked with her to the private outer door and threw a quick glance at the faint glow of light coming from the large upper windows.

'Miss Carstairs waiting up for you, I see!' he muttered, a faint edge in his voice.

'Oh no! She is away until tomorrow!' Nova stated coolly and thoughtlessly. She turned to search for the key, feeling vexed with herself and failed to see the sudden hot gleam in Blanchard's eyes . . .

She raised her long lashes to meet his deep-set gaze.

'Steven—I—er—find that I may after all be interested in your—er—friend's flat!' It was quite truthful, she hadn't said 'for myself' had she? She added a little breathlessly, 'That's if it's still available, of course!'

'Tell you what, let's stand inside and have a last cigarette and we'll talk about it.' His tone was casual and friendly and Nova hid her reluctance, turning to push open the outer door.

It was some degrees warmer in the small porch and Nova unfastened her heavy coat, holding it loosely around her, as a hint that she wanted the talk to be a short one. She refused another cigarette Blanchard offered and waited while he lit his own—she did not like smoking much, and her head still ached from the noise and fug of the party—and possibly the unfinished cigarette stubbed out on an empty plate and popped into her bag.

Blanchard drew on his cigarette, watching the girl through narrowed eyes, sensing her impatience.

'I'm glad that you are interested in a place of your own Nova,' he stated. 'It can be—er—very restricting, sharing a place. My friend's flat is still available. He hasn't had time to place it with an agency yet. How about if I make an appointment for you to meet him and take you to see it?' His smooth tone suddenly revolted Nova—how had she ever thought him worthwhile and dependable?

'Thank you, Steven, but I would much rather just write to him first—or phone!'

'Just as you wish, my dear! I'll be ready to take you over as soon as you set a date. It's only right that as I shall recommend you I should introduce you, eh! Here—I'll jot down his name and phone number on the back of my card.' And at Nova's relieved nod he took his pen from the pocket it shared with tinted glasses and began writing on the back of one of his own cards.

Nova watched in silent amusement as he wrote, thinking of those glasses, which he had worn all evening. The disguise was so superficial as to be useless against anyone knowing him well.

'This light is very poor, isn't it?' he hinted suddenly peering up at the small, dim wall light placed above a narrow shelf.

'I'm sorry, yes, but I really don't think I can ask you . . .' At that moment, from above and far back from the closed inner door, came the distinct sound of a laugh, and very faintly, Sulah's deep miaow.

Even Nova was startled, it was so unexpected, but oh! how welcome!

'Why . . .! Whatever . . .! Surely Eve hasn't stayed at home after all?' She turned an openly relieved face to Steven Blanchard's, and witnessed his obvious fury. A little demon sparked in her eyes. So that had been his game, eh? She really *hadn't* known the real man at all! How had he dared jilt *her*—on the grounds of scandal, when his own undercover life was so obviously questionable? And how *dare* he consider her fair game now? The spark hardened to anger and she took the card from him. He turned to pull open the outer door reluctantly.

'Goodnight, Nova. I'm disappointed we hadn't time for a longer chat, but get in touch with me about the flat, won't you. After all, you will be a personal recommendation!'

He reached out and patted the smooth, cool cheek nearest him and she drew back, saying coldly, 'Thank you. We'll see what happens! Goodnight.' The door closed decisively behind him.

Without waiting for his car to draw away, she let herself in and ran lightly up the stairs.

'Eve,' she called, as she slipped out of her heavy coat in the upper hall. Then picking up her small evening purse containing the all important information for Sue and Ricky, she entered the lounge.

'Darling!' she began, and broke off with a startled cry as a tall, broad figure rose from Eve's big armchair, to face her with a wide grin and twinkling eyes.

'What a gorgeous welcome!' Glencurran

drawled. His eyes went abruptly to the little purse she still held. 'I know you've been to a party, Nova. I hope it was a good one and not the kind one hears of now and then?'

His tone held disapproval and Nova coloured faintly. 'It would not have met with your approval, I am sure,' she answered haughtily, trying to recover her poise. 'It's very nice t-to see you, but I don't quite . . .?' Her voice trailed off as he moved forward, and taking the little purse from her, tossed it on to a nearby table.

'Come and sit down for a moment, and I'll tell you all about it.' He pushed her firmly into the facing chair and Nova, feeling suddenly rather weak in the knees, was glad to sink down.

It took him only minutes to explain things to her. It seemed that he had been able to get away earlier than planned, and on arrival at his hotel, had at once phoned Miss Carstairs. That had been at eight-fifteen. 'Just after I'd gone out,' Nova murmured. Eve had insisted that he come round and make her acquaintance, and they'd made an instant hit with each other. She had left a little later than planned—at nine-thirty, insisting that he await Nova's return.

'Apparently you had intended leaving this— er—party, early? So I decided to wait. I'm glad you've returned, Nova! I wanted to ask you to spend the best part of tomorrow with me! Will you?' He leaned forward and took her small,

148

cool hands in his big grasp, a persuasive smile in the hazel eyes.

Nova had a strange feeling of complete relaxation and well-being, as she returned his gaze. She turned her fingers and clasped them around his and gave a little laugh as his grip tightened eagerly, causing her a sudden excitement.

'Why not?' she replied daringly, adding with a breathless laugh, 'I feel very f-flattered that you want to spend a whole day with me—I really thought that you'd had enough of my company on the island!'

She swayed a little as Glencurran swung her roughly against him, tipping her head back against his arm to look furiously into the lovely eyes. His heart leapt as he noted the enlarged pupils and felt Nova's body in soft, uncontrollable surrender against his.

'Hell's fire,' he cursed fiercely and swung her up into his arms and carried her into the nearest bedroom—luckily her own. She felt as though she was floating on air; the pleasant sensation stayed with her even as Glencurran laid her down none too gently, kneeling beside the bed to raise her again long enough to unzip and pull off her dress. Her shoes followed and then she was being tucked between the sheets. Ross fiercely pushed away the small hands as they clung to his sleeve.

'If I had been anyone else, Nova,' he gritted between clenched teeth, 'I might have taken you in your uncontrolled condition.' And he left her . . .

Nova sank back sleepily, wondering in some confusion if she were drunk—or ill. 'Never wanted a man to hold me l-like that before,' she murmured drowsily, and sank blissfully into heavy dream filled slumber . . .

It was thus Ross found her some twenty minutes later, after screening the open lounge fire, feeding and shutting Sulah in the bathroom where Eve kept his basket and he could exit through a small ventilator on to a sloping roof. Then leaving one or two small lights burning he had gone to check Nova's condition.

She was sleeping heavily, her face flushed, and although her arms were outflung as he gazed he knew that she would have slept off the obvious drug by morning. He found a sheet of pastel-coloured note paper and wrote several lines, propping it where she couldn't fail to see it. He left the room reluctantly, still fighting the urge to rouse the girl to his hungry desire. 'When I do she will know what is happening, and that I am the one she wants— then—then,' he told himself fiercely as he left the flat . . .

He had hesitated about leaving the place, but it had been obvious that Nova would not waken until mid-morning, and Eve had told him of the hourly patrol. Remembering Nova's dreamy, amenable condition, he knew he had

150

done right in leaving, but it hadn't taken much to sum up the intention of the man who had brought her home. He felt murderous, recalling that Nova smoked very rarely indeed.

He fought the murderous rage that rushed over him again with an effort that left beads of sweat on his brow, and his hands clenched on the steering wheel as though it were someone's throat . . .

Chapter Eighteen

Nova's night had started with pleasant dreams and ended with varied and terrifying nightmares. The last one she vaguely remembered, concerning a huge alley cat, who looked like Blanchard, standing over her uttering deep, Siamese type 'miaows', that sounded like 'Niaow! I've *got* you—Niaow!' There was also a persistent clanging sound, which penetrated finally into the last misty edges of sleep, and became reduced to the continuous bleep—bleep—of the bedside phone extension. As she reached out a groping hand to lift the receiver, she heard Sulah's deep-throated protest, faintly, from behind the bathroom door.

The voice that barked at her over the phone, roused her completely.

'Come on, Nova, wakey, wakey! I want you ready by eleven-thirty on the dot! We've a few miles to cover before lunch! Understand?'

'Yes, Ross, I-I'll try, what time is it? Oh!— ten-twenty—well, I'll do my best! Feel a bit headachy, though, and I-I can't quite recall what you are doing here in town? It isn't the tenth until tomorrow, is it?'

'Never mind! I'll remind you in an hour's time. Just get moving, a shower will help the headache and fresh air will do the rest.'

Nova murmured something and hung up shakily. What a bulldozer Glencurran was, and why did she feel so vague about last night's happenings? She recalled clearly, coming home with Blanchard—and the unexpected discovery of Ross in her friend's flat, but from then on—nothing! She scrambled out of bed and threw back the curtains to a clear, cold winter's day with a thin crisp of frost on the shrubs in Eve's small garden.

'I must have been tired,' she said aloud. 'Fancy going to bed in my slip and not even hanging up my dress.' She scowled at it, where it lay, neatly enough, across the back of a tub chair.

Sulah's sad miaow set her rushing to get things organised. 'Before the Laird of Glencurran comes thundering at the door,' she told him, as he fell ravenously on the breakfast she placed down.

She had read the note stating that Glencurran would pick her up and that she was to get a good breakfast—or else . . . !

She was almost ready when the sudden peal of the inner door bell made her jump.

'Good morning, Ross. You are five minutes early, but I'm all ready! Just have to leave a note for Eve in case she returns before us.'

He followed her up the stairs after a brief, close look, ending in a quiet smile as he noted that in spite of faintly shadowed eyes, she looked fit and clear-eyed. Her skin glowed

153

with the soft freshness of a child's and still had that dewy 'straight from the bath' look.

'Eve knows all about it,' he told her laconically, 'and yes, we will be later back, but still in time to have supper with her.'

'Oh! You have it all arranged, haven't you? In that case, I'll get my coat and we'll go.' She sounded slightly piqued, and he hid a grin. 'Still touchy about that precious, new-found independence of hers,' he thought wryly, wondering how she would react to the knowledge of her failure to take care of herself at a 'trendy' party.

Nova checked that Sulah had gone out via his usual route, put down his lunch and a saucer of milk, then allowed Glencurran to help her into her coat. He leaned from behind her and pressed a kiss on to the corner of her mouth and she turned her face up, giving him a shy, uncertain smile. Because of the quizzical look in the keen eyes, she decided it was just a comradely 'peck' and as such should be accepted.

Moments later they had crossed the river and were heading towards Kent. Nova expressed her delight, but informed him wistfully, 'that she hoped he would avoid Meopham, as she'd just sold her father's converted farm-house on the outskirts, and didn't want to torture herself with seeing it again, although the new owner had said she might leave the furniture until after Christmas and she'd have to go then . . .'

'As a matter of fact, you are going to have to face up to it now, because I've bought a small place in that neighbourhood, and I'm to call in on the solicitor handling it for me. They've asked us to tea, and after, you and Mrs Baxter can chat while we wind up my deal.'

'Oh dear! I'll like to meet your business friends, of course, but with any luck your place won't be anywhere near Brambledene! Whereabouts in or near Meopham is it?'

'Oh, the outskirts,' he murmured vaguely, 'but I shan't be viewing it today. Instead we'll go along and have a look at Brambledene . . . immediately after lunch.' He kept his eyes resolutely ahead, concentrating on the heavy traffic.

A protest trembled on Nova's lips, but she proudly held it back. After all, it was foolish to be so chicken-hearted.

Glencurran spun into the car-park of the Cricketers Inn a few minutes before one and Nova gazed around her with suddenly misty eyes. Her parents had liked this place, and she and Mimsey had come here for lunch sometimes, when they were at the farm alone. In spite of the sad memories, she ate a hearty and extremely good lunch; enjoying the friendly service and the pleasant view across the charming village green.

She also chatted more than she realised, and at the end of an hour's eating, Glencurran

155

knew all about Sue and Ricky; their hopes for the flat; Blanchard's part in it, and of her intended visit to sort out some of her mother's things from the farmhouse in this area.

'Eve and I must get it done before the new owner takes over in the new year,' she told him, 'although completion has taken place I understand that I will be given time to get Mother's things out.'

'I can see you are going to be a busy and very well organised girl over the next few weeks! However . . . I shall be back on January the twenty-third and I want you to keep most of that week free for me . . . please!' hastily disarming the little spark that had sprung up in the lovely eyes at his naturally autocratic tone.

'I'll think about it,' she responded coolly and then spoiled it by laughing. 'You *do* have a way of demanding!' she told him with mock severity.

They set off again soon after and she was able to direct him to Moordown Lane, at the end of which, he pulled up before the charming black and white farmhouse that Nova had always held so dear. She had the key on her keyring and with misty eyes and lips that insisted on a slight tremble, quickly controlled, she opened the front door and led him in.

'It's a gem,' he agreed sombrely, after they had browsed all over it for an hour.

Nova sighed shakily. 'I'm glad I came now,

156

after all! Mother had hoped that she and Dad would retire here one day.' She raised shadowed eyes to his searching glance. 'Thank you, for once again making me face up to things,' she whispered.

His mouth twisted wryly, but he bent and kissed her swiftly on the lips, then took her firmly to the door. 'If I'm to stay in this area from time to time, you may see it again,' he said quietly.

The rest of the day passed swiftly and Nova was relieved to find herself recovering quickly from the depression she had felt when they'd left Brambledene. The Baxters were a pleasant, early middle-aged couple, and she enjoyed Edna Baxter's company throughout the time they were left to entertain each other. It seemed they knew Henry Balfour quite well and that Ross had been at school with Ian Baxter's younger brother, now in practice in Glasgow.

'Clive and his wife come to us for a couple of weeks every summer, so it's to be hoped that his visit will coincide with Ross's stay in the district,' Edna told an interested Nova. She didn't like to ask exactly where that would be, knowing that Ross would tell her sooner or later. It might even be that she would know the place . . .

By six-thirty Glencurran headed the car Londonwards, grinning down at a well tucked up girl, her glowing face framed in the fur-trimmed hood of vivid yellow, matching the warm coat.

Stopping only for dinner at the Tiger's Head in Chislehurst; a good meal to which they both again did full justice, they arrived back at the shop a few minutes after nine, to find a welcoming Eve awaiting them.

'Well dears, did you have a good time . . .' she began and caught a warning glance above Nova's dark head 'In Kent and at the Baxters?' she ended more cautiously.

'You *were* in the picture, Eve dear,' the unaware girl laughed. 'I can see that you and Mr Glen—er—Ross, really hit it off!' Her laughing eyes expressed complete satisfaction.

They sat exchanging news happily for an hour and then Eve, on her way to make coffee, remembered, 'Oh, Nova! I forgot, Sue and Ricky phoned to ask if you'd had any luck getting that address?'

Nova jumped to her feet. 'I'd forgotten it too!' she said. 'It's in my silver purse. I'll get it.' She returned almost at once, the card given her by Blanchard held in slim finger tips. It reminded her that Glencurran had given her only a brief and somehow, not quite satisfactory explanation of her homecoming last night.

The name on the card was Glen Randell and the phone number was a Fulham one.

'Is that the Glen Randell I met at your guest-house, Ross?' she asked in surprise. 'If

158

so . . . what a strange coincidence!'

'I think it must be! He lives off the Fulham Road. I knew he was to be married soon, but not that he would be moving! He lives at home weekends, with his father and aunt . . . the housekeeper tyrant—Oh! you've heard of her?' with an amused grin at Nova's dimple. 'If it is, then, of course, I know him well and can fix a meeting for you . . .'

'No . . . *please*, Ross!' she broke in proudly, 'let me manage it now that I have his name and number. They are *my* friends and it did take quite an effort on my part to approach Steven for it!'

She caught her breath at the suddenly bleak look in his eyes, and even flinched at his short, violent movement.

'All right, little Nova! You go ahead and do it on your own. I shouldn't have butted in, but I'd be grateful if you'd let me run you and the—er—happy couple over to view the flat . . . if and when you get permission?' He smiled disarmingly, the coldness gone from his eyes and mouth, and Nova agreed eagerly. She did not realise that she had unwittingly given him the fact that Blanchard had been her escort last night, although he had guessed instinctively . . .

The remainder of his visit passed with incredible speed following a well-planned pattern divided between business and pleasure. He took her to dinner twice and then

159

a third time with Eve; they spent an evening with Miles Tremayne and the following one taking Ricky and Sue to look over the flat in a quiet side road off the Fulham Road.

Glen Randell remembered Nova at once. He showed them over his compact domain with a warm friendliness. First, a roomy lounge, then a slightly smaller bedroom; a well-equipped small kitchen and last, a tiny bathroom. It also had its own back door to a garden staircase leading from a roomy landing. Sue, usually so calm and tough, was almost beside herself with delight. They assured Glen Randell that Ricky had started a good job with the Cunard shipping line and that Sue, herself, was to do a part time job as secretary to a local solicitor, and help a friend with a small boutique at weekends.

He, in turn, agreed to leave certain fundamental items of furniture leaving them free to add their own personal touches. Throughout this exchange, Ross had stood back coolly; smiling only as Nova, the introductions made, joined him as spectator also. He did insist however, that they celebrate with a quick pint in the Rembrandt. Here they were joined later by Glen and his fiancée Sheila, and the evening ended very pleasantly.

In no time at all, Nova was bidding Ross goodbye. She was startled to find an ache in her throat and a certain reluctance at his going. She even returned his goodbye kiss in an affectionate way that set his teeth on edge and almost had him shaking her into awareness of himself as a man. Had he been aware that she was only too dangerously aware of him; of his strength; his domination over her own less forceful character, and of his increasing power to make her waver from her intense determination to prove herself able to stand very firmly alone, he would no doubt have uttered a wild rebel yell and whipped her up with him on to the plane and back to Glencurran Castle.

She did allow herself to express regret that he would not be with them for Christmas.

'So do I,' he assured her grimly, 'but I'll be back in January remember and I shall phone you at Miles's on Boxing Day as arranged. One word of warning, little Nova . . .' an edge crept into his voice and his grip on her upper arms tightened, 'keep away from Blanchard!'

For a brief moment the usual defiance leapt into the wide eyes raised to his, then sensing a certain urgency behind the order, she nodded mutely.

Across the top of her head he saw Eve Carstairs returning from where she had been chatting to a friend who had arrived on an earlier plane. He bent his dark red head and pressed a hard, last kiss on the rosy mouth and a few moments later he was gone . . .

Nova was unusually silent on the return trip to town, and Eve, handling her car expertly but cautiously along the busy road from the airport left her alone until the girl herself felt ready to chat. Nova threw her a grateful smile, realising her friend's forbearance and leaning back, gave herself up to thinking back over the last eight days.

She had seen little of Ross during most days after their Sunday outing, which she had enjoyed so very much in spite of her first reluctance to see her favourite home.

During the following week, their dates together had been lively and completely enjoyable. He had met her young friends, Emmy and Geoff; been very helpful with Ricky and Sue; and most important to her just now, had developed an immediate and special liking for her dear Eve. Eve had taken to him also, she was sure; their easy and relaxed manner with each other was obvious. A little smile lit her eyes and she turned warmly to the quiet, mature woman by her side.

'Eve darling! I'm looking forward to Christmas, but even more to the end of January!' she said breathlessly, and Eve laughed, her understanding complete.

'He is certainly something, isn't he?' was all she said.

'He certainly is . . . do you know, he practically *ordered* me not to see Steven Blanchard again?'

'I'm not surprised!' Eve answered drily. 'I can't see how that nice young Mr Randell knew him so well?'

'Neither did Ross! But in his usual fashion he went straight to the point . . . and asked. It seems Glen met him through their travel agency and was only an acquaintance whom Steven was taking advantage of. As he'd recommended quite a few customers to them, Glen had gone out of his way to be obliging. Luckily for Ricky and Sue eh? But in spite of Ross's *order*, I must at least have the courtesy to phone and say thank you to Steven; after all, he did put me on to it! I won't get involved any further with him though!' And looking at the firm set of the curving mouth, Eve believed her . . .

Chapter Nineteen

Nova went round helping Eve tidy and pack away the smaller objects left after a very busy week. It was Christmas Eve and they were to close at midday, in a few minutes in fact. The last cabinet locked and all doors secured, they made their way up to a flat bright and welcoming with firelight; great vases of pine sprays and holly; a gay display of Christmas cards received, and a daintily set luncheon-table. Mrs Bowden was certainly a treasure . . .

Lunch cleared away, the two of them set about preparing as much as possible for tomorrow's main meal for Eve was to entertain at home. 'For the first time in about seven years,' she informed Nova happily. Miles, Sara and her 'friend' were to come; also the friend whom Eve had visited at Wimbledon on that strange weekend.

By six o'clock they had had enough, so by mutual agreement they prepared a sizeable late tea, after which Eve prepared to meet the Dinsdales at a show they had booked together. Nova set off to keep a supper date at the Good Earth, a very popular Chinese restaurant in the Kings Road, chosen by Ricky, Sue, Emmy, Geoff and Tod, when she had asked them to let her stand them all supper as a Christmas gift.

Emmy and Geoff were waiting for her on the corner as she left the flat at eight sharp, and with a lifting of spirits she joined them, then they walked on together, chatting happily.

When Tod dropped her off outside the flat again, it was just gone midnight. She scrambled from the 'old banger', clutching a huge box of very expensive petits fours for which they had pooled together, and wishing them a final, 'Goodnight and a very happy Christmas,' a tired Nova let herself in quietly. She was first in, however, and had time to place her gift to Eve by the clock on Eve's bedside table, and to leave a hot drink prepared, before turning in.

She remembered no more until nine o'clock, when Eve's quiet movements from the kitchen faintly penetrated her last moments of sleep. For a while she lay remembering the previous Christmas. She and her father had entertained friends on the day, and on Boxing Day had gone to Steven's home, where his parents, whilst making them welcome, had seemed uneasy in the presence of their only son, who did not live at home on a permanent basis. Recalling this, Nova frowned a little: no use to puzzle about it now, it no longer concerned her. She had phoned her thanks for his help over that flat and had very firmly refused his insistence that she have dinner with him soon.

For the rest of the day Nova was so busy and

relatively happy, that even her sad memories dimmed into the background of her mind.

After a late dinner, Sara, whose 'friend' had turned out to be Ian, took her into Eve's bedroom and handed her a very large box, which they had somehow smuggled in without her knowledge.

As they had all exchanged gifts earlier, Nova raised wondering eyes to her friend's sparkling face.

'Oh, go on, Nova! Do please open it quickly, I'm longing to see what it is!'

Nova obliged with trembling fingers and with Sara's help lifted out a beautiful, mid-calf-length plaid coat, trimmed with softest pale grey fur at hem, cuffs and collar. A tiny cossack style hat to match was included; but the thing that made Nova catch her breath . . . *this* was one of her very own plaid designs . . . a gorgeous blend of soft over-checks of lilac, pink, black and oatmeal!

Her stunned eyes met Sara's, then she turned to open the box, first taking up a gift card which stated simply: 'From Ross' . . . then a long brown envelope. Inside, a typed business letter stated precisely that the firm of 'Glencurran Tweeds' were pleased to accept two of the first three designs offered, and to consider the further sketches recently brought in by Mr Glencurran.

There was also a substantial cheque enclosed.

Nova spent the remainder of the holiday period in a daze, from which she emerged long enough on Boxing Day to hug Sara and Ian ecstatically when they announced their engagement.

'Actually—before we came here,' Sara admitted shyly, 'but Ian wanted to get the ring here—in town.' She displayed a lovely opal and diamond ring happily, and Ian's eyes dwelt on her glowing face with the light of deep content in them.

Later, Glencurran phoned as he had said he would and listened to her stammered thanks with a frustration that had him clenching his powerful fist, because he was not beside her, able to watch the shyness and delight that would be mingled in the violet-blue depths of her eyes, or to crush the stammering words to silence beneath his kiss. Before ending the call, he issued an invitation to a special tweed display to be held at a well-known West End store during the first week of February.

'I want to take you for a special reason Nova, so I shall send on the official invitation card although of course, you will be there as my guest.'

His voice held all its old deep-toned arrogance and for a short-lived moment of rebellion Nova almost laid claim to a previous engagement. Her own innate honesty, coupled with a genuine curiosity won however, and she accepted, albeit a little coolly.

During the following week, she and Eve were able to motor down to Kent, as the light crisp frosts over Christmas had given way to a blowy wetness, just a few degrees milder. At the end of their visit, Nova had sorted out several of her mother's favourite pieces including a charming little display cabinet, which Eve said was eighteenth century and probably by William Kent; a Queen Anne knee-hole writing-desk; a panelled oak coffer, which Eve thought to be late seventeenth century; a pair of charming Hepplewhite armchairs, with heart-shaped backs; two of the family group pictures of which Mimsey had been so fond, one by Hardy and one by Zoffany; several pieces of Spode; a lovely set of nineteenth century fish plates with shell-shaped recesses, and a small collection of early Waterford crystal.

All these Eve promised to store for her until a later date, and they were carefully packed and seen safely off to London. The remainder was fairly valued; some to be disposed of to customers personally recommended by Eve; the rest to be offered to the new owners through Henry Balfour.

Tired and a little depressed at the contact with old memories, Nova was glad to get back into the busy routine of everyday life again.

She found Sue and Ricky, a quiet wedding day behind them, already happily settled into their new flat, when she and Eve went along at their invitation one evening. They took along a generous bale of household linen and were more than rewarded when Sue fell on it with a squeal of delight. Even Ricky expressed warm approval of the gay modern designs, 'Yeah. Way out man—er—girls. Thanks a lot!'

Eve raised a comical eyebrow at being classed as a girl, but even so, she found many mutual points of interest with the younger people during the evening and Nova realised how very much her efforts at independence had been helped by her old friend's support and understanding.

Then, suddenly, it was the last week in January and she and Eve were putting the final touches to dinner for four as Miles Tremayne was to join Eve, Ross and herself for the evening.

It had been snowing for the last two days. A thin, light covering over London had seemed to take the city back two hundred years when viewed from certain aspects and Ross, used to extremely hard weather, found it rather charming in spite of its inconvenience. His satisfaction with things in general was complete when Nova opened the door to him a few minutes before seven-thirty.

For a moment he allowed himself a long eager gaze at the girl, as with eyes shining warmly with obvious pleasure at his arrival, she stepped shyly to one side for him to enter. In the soft light of the tiny lower hall, she looked enchanting; wearing again the pale grey velvet dress swirling gently to her ankles, a heavy silver belt, little silver slippers and again the lovely amethyst and diamond brooch he had given her. Ross found himself hard put to it to control his need to crush her, bear-like in his arms.

He made do with a firm grip on the rounded chin, and an equally firm kiss on the smiling mouth.

The quiet dinner which followed was so pleasant, they all four sat longer over it than they had intended; so when Ross suggested that Eve and Miles settle by a glowing fire whilst he and Nova did the washing-up, Eve, after only a mild protest that her Mrs Bowden would tackle it in the morning, laughingly gave in.

'I think he wants an excuse to be alone with Nova,' she told Miles, quite unnecessarily, as he was fully aware of Ross's intentions.

Nova tied a frilly apron round her trim waist and smiled up at the tall, powerfully built man standing at ease at one end of the sink unit, a gay tea-towel at the ready; a glow in his clear eyes, which deepened as her gaze met his. She turned hastily to the basin, turning on taps and adding washing-up liquid with nervous abandon.

'This r-reminds me of the i-island . . . when you and I used to s-stand in for Meg,' she stammered, her head held low.

'Ay! We were quite a good team . . . once you'd recognised who was boss,' was the laconic, arrogant answer.

The black curls flew out as she turned her head indignantly, her eyes sparkling with temper. 'Ross Glencurran . . .' she began, 'you are an overbearing man! . . .'

'I know, and you little Nova, are delightfully easy to rouse—thank goodness!' His eyes met hers wickedly. 'That's broken the ice hasn't it, my sweet? I felt you gather a cloak of "keep out" crystals around you as soon as we left the lounge.'

Nova let out her breath with a laugh. 'Oh dear! Yes, it's true Ross. You see, I want to say a very special thank you for so many things; this lovely brooch again; my wonderful coat; the cheque for my designs . . . and oh, so many things! But I didn't want you to get the wrong idea—I—I . . .' her eyes pleaded for understanding.

Glencurran stacked the dry dishes carefully before spreading the tea-towel across its rail. Nova, running the suds away saw with regret and no little trepidation that his eyes were cold again, his jaw stern and set. She wasn't surprised when he spun her round, holding her firmly before him.

'Are you trying to say that you are still allowing your pride to come between us; that you haven't forgiven me for being on hand at the time of your greatest despair?' He shook her none too gently. 'Don't you know that my extravagant claim to your life was made purely to rouse your fighting spirit? Have I succeeded too well, Nova? Do you hate me so much, that you won't even consider handing me your life?'

Nova lifted her palms against his broad chest, closing her eyes against the harshness of his face. From the lounge, faintly, she could hear the sound of music. 'Please God,' she prayed, 'don't let Eve come in yet. I must make him understand.'

'Well?' His voice came sternly, and she winced as the grip on her upper arms tightened.

'Oh, Ross! No! No! Of course I don't hate you. I—I did at first . . . on the island, you know! But . . . yes . . . call it pride if you like! I *have* to prove to you that I can manage my own life and that's what I'm doing . . .'

'You weren't making a very good job of it on the night of December the eighth,' he gritted, and at once knew he had erred. In his despair and hurt, he had only given her cause for more distress. He cursed himself for a clumsy fool.

'W-what do you mean?' she whispered, apprehension in her eyes and voice.

He put her on a kitchen chair, then crossed to lock the door. 'In for a penny . . . ,' he quoted angrily, then straddled a chair before her.

'Nova, I had meant to tell you this at a much

172

later date when you and I had settled things between us! Now, it must be explained fully. In a few more days the police will be making an arrest. Someone you've known very well.' He motioned her to silence, and went on, 'It will be in all the papers then but I wasn't sure how you'd take it! That's why I'd hoped to have you accept me tonight! I made a clumsy mess of it, which in itself is sickening. I usually keep my head in all emergencies.' He scowled heavily.

'Are y-you referring to Steven Blanchard? W-what has h-he done?'

'Yes, I am . . . he is wanted for drug handling!' At the harsh words Nova uttered a little cry, covering her white face with shaking hands.

'T-that's why I couldn't recall that night very clearly,' she whispered. 'If y-you hadn't been there, he would have tried to c-come up to the f-flat . . .' Her voice shook with horror and Glencurran felt a surge of satisfaction that at least he had been the one to put the police on Blanchard's track, with the aid of the half-smoked cigarette given her by Blanchard just before leaving that party . . .

He stood up now and pulled her up into his arms. 'Forget it, sweetheart! I was there, thank God! Forgive me for being so clumsy tonight. I'd hoped for so much! My own fault—I'm a brute! Come on, dry your tears and splash with cold water or Eve and Miles will think I've been beating you.' He tipped her face up and gently kissed the damp cheeks. 'Perhaps one day, you'll be brave enough to come and tell me that your pride isn't so important after all, but that I am? That day can't come soon enough for *me*!'

'If only *you* weren't present at all my greatest humiliations! I feel so—so—*'shamed!'* she whispered against his chest and felt his arms close strongly.

'Thank God it *was* me,' he thought grimly, and proceeded to help her restore the ravages of the last half an hour.

It was over an hour after leaving it that they returned to the lounge to be tactfully welcomed back by the seniors.

Eve's shrewd eyes took in her young friend's paleness, as also did Miles' professional gaze.

Glencurran anticipated both looks. 'It was surprisingly cool out there,' he murmured. 'May I pour drinks for us all, Miss Carstairs?'

'Please do. We waited for you both.'

Ten minutes later the drink and the warmth had restored Nova's colour as well as her equilibrium, to Glencurran's great relief. She put on such a good show that Eve and Miles found themselves readily accepting his explanation.

'Well done, little Nova,' he murmured against her cheek as he kissed her goodnight. 'You've more than proved to *my* satisfaction over many weeks, that you can stand firmly on your own two small feet. Hurry and satisfy yourself—*please* sweetheart.'

She shook her head gently. 'It isn't very easy for me—but I will try—I promise!'

He knew that for the moment that would have to do. He had only himself to blame for tonight's set-back. Aloud he merely said, 'Don't forget our lunch date on Tuesday, and the show on Wednesday!'

They were to see a popular show in the West End, taking Eve and Miles as their guests.

That night Nova lay sleepless for a long time; reliving every moment from the time she had found her father lying in a pool of his own blood; her rejection by Blanchard, and the shocked flight to Ardslignish; her first awareness of Glencurran on the island of Curransay and the swift spark of hatred kindled by his arbitrary treatment. Then later, her stay with Lossie, and her short stay at Glencurran Castle. Finally, her return to London and her own determined efforts to sort out her affairs and make a new independent life for herself.

She tossed wearily, turning to switch on her little bedside light then lay gazing round the pleasant bedroom, so tastefully furnished by Eve. 'But not my own' a persistent voice whispered. Then she wondered, 'Was there really such a thing as *complete* independence?

Are we not all a little involved with each other, either through business contacts, friendship or love?' She had been so busy since leaving Scotland, finding forgetfulness and pleasure in both her work and social contacts. She had almost recovered from her deep-seated resentment of Ross; growing steadily more aware of him as an attractive and attentive man and one who, moreover, obviously found *her* very desirable! But did he really love her? Or was it just that he felt he had the right to take over her life after such intimate involvement with it? If only she could sink that awful pride and ask him outright . . . !

The old tide of resentment swept over her again as she pummelled her pillow vigorously. 'Why does he always have to be around when things go wrong,' she muttered, then felt sick with shame at the unfairness of her remark.

If he had not been, she would not now be here and—a little shudder ran through her—if it had been Blanchard and not Glencurran—alone here with her . . . !

'God! I was so far gone—I couldn't have done a thing! It must have been Ross who put me to bed!' Remembering the scanty slip she awoke in the next morning, she coloured hotly. How angry he had been in the kitchen; she might never have known, but for his outburst!

'Not surprising, my girl!' she told herself severely. 'After all his goodness to you, too! Oh, well! I shall have to make up my own mind what to do eventually,' and she flicked off the light and made a determined effort to get to sleep . . .

Chapter Twenty

Nova spent the following evening with the young Blaines, returning with them to the house next door to her old home for a brief supper with Peggy's parents. She was able to chat quite cheerfully about old times; explaining that she had met the new owners of Number Four a couple of times in Henry Balfour's office.

'I've met the people who have bought the little house in Brighton also, and I'm glad to say that they are perfectly willing to buy the furnishings and fittings,' Nova explained brightly.

Mr and Mrs Pleydell expressed sympathy and interest, asking how the sale of Brambledene was progressing.

'Oh! It's completed, but I haven't met the new owner yet.' She smiled calmly, and shortly after Peggy and Robert took her back to the shop.

'Thank you for a nice evening, and please thank your parents again for me, I so enjoyed seeing them once more, Peggy.'

In no time at all the afternoon of the tweed show had arrived and Eve, having decided to close the shop—'such a slack period anyway'—they had plenty of time to get ready.

They were to make their own way to Bond

Street, as Ross, whom Nova had not seen since Wednesday when they'd seen a delightful musical together, was so busy with business involvements.

She was to have dinner with him that evening, and possibly once more, before he returned to Scotland on Saturday . . . only three more days.

Nova realised that over the past months, she had grown more and more to look forward to his 'comings', and to regret his 'goings', but never had she felt so strangely bereft as she did now, at the thought of the approaching parting!

'It'll be all right once he's gone,' she told herself uneasily. 'I'll have so much to do—and anyway he'll be back for two weeks at Whitsun, and of course, I shall see him at Sara and Ian's wedding the weekend before Easter. I can't deny that I am learning to miss him! He's such good company always!' But she knew she hadn't always thought so, and that it had become much more than that . . .

Eve drove the car cautiously through the dirty slush that had been a crisp blanket of white only two days ago; wondering, as everyone always did, why the city dwellers never seemed to be prepared for bad weather and still did their best to rush around in spite of it.

Nova was recalling that the moans and groans of the general public had amused Ross.

'A timely reminder that man cannot always have his way. Nature still has the last word and I hope she always will in the elemental order of things.'

His deep laugh had brought a responsive dimple to her mouth.

A little after three o'clock, she and Eve were shown to ultra modern chairs at the back of four semicircles of seats. In spite of the bad conditions outside, a great many people seemed to be present, and the hum of conversation filled the warm, scented air.

Three smart waitresses were serving drinks and biscuits, but they disappeared discreetly as an elegant silver-haired woman stepped through the softly draped, ivory silk curtains at the back of a small podium. The hum of voices faded as the alert and keen-eyed faces of buyers, designers and a few reporters focussed on the speaker. She announced clearly, in a soft, cultured voice, that they were to see a collection of spring and autumn garments in beautiful Glencurran Tweeds, and that she would be introducing a lovely new set of designs not yet made into garments as they were so new.

A little ripple of interest ran round the great room and then the show began. Eve and Nova, like most women of all ages would be, found themselves readily absorbed in the delightful display of suits, topcoats, capes, trouser suits and even tweed covered handbags, most of the display in plaid designs.

At last the silver-haired mistress of ceremonies stepped forward with raised hand to still the ripple of applause. Nova seized the moment to look around for Ross, feeling surprisingly disappointed that he did not appear to be present to witness the success of his show.

With half her mind she heard the announcement, 'And now, ladies and gentlemen, we have six new tweeds to show you—some of them so fine and dainty that they would make up easily into evening dresses. We are going to show you three designs in a heavy version and three designs in an ultra fine, very light version. All of them by a new young designer, with the misty magic of the Highlands very much in mind . . .! I give you Glencurran's "Nova Tweeds."' With a dramatic flourish she stepped back, motioning towards the far corner of the room, where another ivory silk drape parted to reveal a slowly moving dais.

Nova stared as one in a dream as the dais came slowly into the centre of the semicircle and stopped. She and Eve gazed at each other in stunned amazement as they saw eager buyers reach out and finger the beautifully draped swathes of woollen tweed. She heard comments on the unusual blending of pastels, and the daring of the more vivid shades, and could believe neither her eyes nor her ears.

181

Then, clearly, above the rest, a sharply critical voice stated, 'Oh, yes! Lovely, I grant you; but I doubt if the colours used in these heavier qualities would look well made up as—well topcoats, for instance!'

'Oh! but they would and *do*, sir! Let me show you!' And to her own horror Nova found herself walking proudly forward towards the podium, mounting the three shallow steps and posing with as much charm and grace—and certainly a better figure—as any professional model.

For some reason, heaven blessed, she had put on for the first time, the lovely coat, with its little cossack hat. She had searched diligently for soft knee-high boots, gloves, and a handbag to match the pale grey fur edging on coat and hat. The result was devastating. She tossed the blue-black curls and with sparkling eyes, induced by a mingled excitement and anger, she twirled slowly around as she had watched the models do for the past hour.

The man standing well back near the entrance arch, stared with glowing eyes and thrusting jaw. Then with slow strides, he moved forward to leap lightly, for all his size, to stand by the girl. His gaze held the startled eyes briefly, then, taking her hand he said, 'Ladies and gentlemen, let me introduce you to Miss Nova Helmann, the lovely designer of "Nova Tweeds." She makes a great model too, doesn't she?' With a note of laughter that brought a responsive echo from his intrigued audience.

* * *

'Eve darling . . . I can't imagine what possessed me to do such a thing!' Nova whispered in disbelief later.

It was six-thirty and they had just finished a slightly belated tea. Since Glencurran had taken her back to Eve and then seen them to the main entrance of the great store, Nova had been in a state of nervous apprehension. It had been made worse by the fact that he had said nothing—merely—'I'll see *you* later on, young lady!' in a deeply ominous voice. She had failed to see the wicked grin he'd exchanged with Eve, above her head.

'Now, pet! Don't fret yourself so! It was a grand gesture and I'm sure that Glencurran Tweeds will profit greatly by it. You weren't treading on any professional toes, my dear. You did it freely, and wearing your own garments! Now stop worrying, dear, and go and get ready. Ross will be here in an hour.'

When Nova came breathlessly into the lounge just after seven-thirty, it was to find Glencurran already there. He finished the small whisky and soda Eve had given him, then turned to survey the flushed face and the hurried breathing of the girl before him.

183

'I can see you've had a rush to get ready,' he stated coolly, adding sardonically, 'Or dare I hope that this agitation is because you are pleased to be coming out with me?'

Nova's chin lifted proudly. 'Both!' she told him shortly and went swiftly to kiss Eve goodnight.

His eyes sparked, but he said nothing and moments later they were on their way. He had booked a table at the Barrie Room, at the Kensington Palace Hotel. It was delightfully warm, tasteful and very luxurious, and Nova relaxed a little as they were shown to a quiet corner table by a pleasant and courteous maitre d'hotel.

With a healthy young appetite, she went into raptures over the exceptionally good food served.

'I'm going to have to watch you, my lassie, or you'll not be doing any more modelling for me!' Then abruptly, 'Why did you, Nova?'

She coloured and met his eyes nervously. 'I—I don't really know, Ross! It—it was that man's tone of voice, I think!' A surprised note entered her voice. 'Also—I felt—that I was defending you and your judgement in some way!'

Her puzzled look set his pulses racing.

'Is it that you might be ready to say yes, Nova?' he suggested hopefully.

She met his quizzical look bravely. 'I—I want to,' she whispered, twirling her wine glass round between slim fingers. 'But—but there's something I'm not sure about . . . Something missing!' Her voice held bewilderment.

His powerful brown hand reached across the table and gripped hers, stopping its fidgeting.

'Is it this, little Nova . . .? I love you—deeply . . . and I need you—badly!' The clear, hard eyes held hers with an intensity that made her quake. Then—it was as though a door had opened.

'That's it! That's what I *longed* to hear, that you *loved* . . . and needed me! Oh, Ross . . . darling! Yes! Yes! Yes!' Her face was radiant, her voice shook.

The grip tightened painfully and she warned, 'Mind the glass darling, *please*,' with a little laugh, her eyes suddenly shy again.

They left earlier than planned so that they could have an hour or so alone in the flat to make plans. Not that Nova had much to say in the matter. Glencurran took a moment only to break open the banked fire: then seated himself before it, in Eve's most accommodating armchair, reaching to tumble her on to his lap.

'Just repeat that Yes! Yes! Yes! and give me time to kiss you soundly between each one,' he ordered arrogantly, and Nova obeyed meekly. The last Yes! was very shaky indeed and almost inaudible.

'All right, you can get your breath back

while I tell you my plans. I hope, sweetheart,' he added belatedly, 'that they will please you?' She nodded mutely, tipping her head back against his shoulder, content just to listen for now.

'Right! We shall get officially engaged at once! We'll get a nice ring tomorrow. We shall announce our wedding date at Sara's wedding. Suit you so far?' Again the silent nod, but a small hand moved timidly to push back the obstinate dark red curl that would spring over one strongly marked eyebrow. He captured the slim hand and pressed his lips into the soft palm.

'Don't distract me!' he said sternly, then, 'I thought we'd marry at Whitsun and spend three weeks honeymooning at a nice little place I bought recently.'

'Oh?' Nova sat upright and raised delicate eyebrows. 'Whitsun . . .? Well! it doesn't give me very long—and whereabouts is this place? N-not the one in Kent, is it?'

'It gives you plenty of time to tie up your affairs here, Nova!' he stated implacably. 'As to the other question; yes, it is in Kent! Can't you take it?'

She met his hard gaze defiantly for a mere second. 'Oh, Ross! Darling—yes! Anywhere with you . . . but I had thought . . . perhaps the island?'

His arms enclosed her like a vice. 'Do you know you are the most wonderful girl! Here I am, still doubting your courage and you floor me with a remark like that! Sweetheart . . . I am a brute!' His mouth crushed hers to silence when she tried to protest at his harsh judgement of himself. He raised his head at last, a stunned look in his eyes.

'The place I had in mind,' he told her hoarsely, 'was called Brambledene and . . .'

He broke off in surprise as Nova, with a gasp, buried her face in his dinner jacket and burst into tears.

It took him twenty minutes to soothe away the tears; invoking a watery smile at last by saying, 'Now that's enough! Eve will be in soon and she'll think I make a habit of causing you to weep.' He rocked her gently a short while longer, and then suggested they get coffee under way.

By the time Eve returned, he had agreed, with arrogant generosity, to spending their honeymoon on the island and a later holiday—or 'perhaps even Christmas?'—at Brambledene.

Eve, hearing their quiet laughter, came in search of them, and entered to find a radiant girl standing within the circle of Glencurran's arms. She broke free and turned to her old friend with shy delight.

'Eve darling! Guess what?' Her eyes sparkled with mischief, as she took Ross's big hand in hers. He leaned swiftly downwards from his great height and with supreme assurance, calmly kissed the white neck, then slid an arm around her waist again.

'It doesn't need much guessing, my children!' Eve laughed. 'I'll—er—go ahead with the coffee, which I see is just ready—and you two can follow with the biscuits.' She lifted the small tray, threw them a warm, approving smile and walked out.

Ross pulled Nova into his arms again, smoothing the tumbled curls. 'Know what,' he drawled, 'you do look as though you've been proposed to . . . and as though you've accepted!' His eyes moved to her mouth again and she forestalled his intention hastily.

'We *two*,' she stated firmly, 'are to follow with the biscuits.'

'Right! I can wait a few minutes,' he assured her outrageously and picked up the plate meekly enough—for the present.

But the light in his eyes promised retribution.

Chapter Twenty-One

The girl stood poised at the very edge of the tiny wooden jetty for a split second; then she dived with smooth grace into the cold waters of Loch Sunart. The man watching her so closely showed strong teeth in a rather self-satisfied grin which broke into open laughter as the girl's head emerged in its white petal cap, gasping.

'Why are the loch waters always so icy?' she called and a moment later he too, plunged to emerge a few feet away, shaking his head.

'Good for you, darling! Come on, get moving!' And he struck out along the edge of Curransay with powerful overarm strokes followed at a slower pace by Nova. She was a fairly good swimmer, but as Glencurran drew easily away and was obviously intending to make for the point, she abandoned the effort to keep up and turned towards the tiny sandy cove. Here, she quickly towelled her tingling limbs, then dressed in the yellow linen slacks and matching sun top which was more than adequate for the warmth of this lovely, early June day.

She threw a look out to where Ross's head and arms could be seen, flashing in the bright sun, as he neared the point, then she turned and scrambled her way to the top of the little point, from which—it seemed so long ago—she had once called frantically for help . . .

Having reached the point, Glencurran rolled on to his back, resting briefly; his brilliant eyes searching back along the water's edge for Nova's white cap. No sign of her! 'Given up,' he thought without worry. One of his orders with regard to swimming in the loch had been, 'Never attempt more than you can manage easily.' He had not doubted that his order would be obeyed.

As he rolled into powerful action again, his eye caught sight of the vivid figure outlined against the sky and shrubs at the top of the point.

He trod water and waved back at her before turning back towards the jetty.

'It won't take him long to get up here,' the girl smiled to herself, 'and I'll bet he will be ravenous.' She dropped to her knees and began to arrange the picnic tea Ross had carried up earlier, covering it with a plastic sheet to await his arrival.

The sheltered spot was ideal, the turf warm to her touch and she lay face down, drowsily relaxed, thinking of the events of the past nine months which had led to these last three weeks of supreme happiness. A happiness which her innermost heart told her, would last for the rest of their lives together.

How pleased for her everyone had been, especially her own few but staunch friends.

She had stayed at Glencurran for a few days after Sara and Ian's wedding; getting to know the people on the estate and farms; gaining in experience and assurance with every moment.

Under Ross's watchful eyes they had spent a day at the factory at Fort Augustus. This she had enjoyed very much, having a personal interest now in the making of fine tweed. Only one incident had marred the pleasure of that day, she recalled now, one youngish man had shown open coldness to her; had even been a little rude and she had not known how to cope with it, feeling again lost and unsure. Ross had sternly put her straight.

'Nova, you must learn to take the rough with the smooth! Not everyone can like you. Either learn to ignore it or if the case warrants it—fight back! Ted Clarke happens to be our designer. I think your very good efforts in that direction constitute a mild threat to him!' He had given her his clear, hard look, which she returned bravely; then he had ordered brusquely, 'Handle him firmly, but with tact, my lassie, and don't worry as to whether he likes you or not. It's ay more important that he respects you!'

Later, they had taken a few members of the staff for drinks and she had, with renewed confidence, made the opportunity to have a few words alone with Ted Clarke.

'Your designs are beautiful,' she told him sincerely, adding calmly and honestly, 'I do hope to submit some of my own from time to time. It won't be often, of course, perhaps once a year, and I don't suppose they will be accepted! Being his wife will not influence the boss in any way.' Her laugh had been genuine and Clarke had grinned reluctantly in response.

'I've yet tae meet the person who could soft soap the boss into doing somethin' he wasnae ready to!' he admitted and on this note of mutual understanding they parted.

She had met Clarke again just before their wedding day and his attitude of cool respect had well satisfied Ross.

They had married from the Castle, leaving during the reception for Curransay, now almost three weeks ago. Meg and Jock had been given a 'bonus' holiday, so that she and Ross could spend their honeymoon alone and even now, Nova's face flushed at the memory of the first few days getting to know the depth of Ross's love.

'It will take me a lifetime to get used to his arrogance that can turn to tenderness in a heartbeat of time, and he has taught me so much. It's wonderful to know that I can always depend on his strength and his love and yet, at the same time, to know that I have a self-reliance of my own that would enable me to stand by him—in any emergency—*if* the need arose! I *might* even—one day—be able to *manage* him!' And at the delicious but improbable thought, her mouth curved and she dozed off.

Glencurran stood for several moments gazing at his young wife, sleeping like a child; her softly flushed cheek pressed on to one hand, the other, lying with curled fingers above her head. The afternoon sun struck golden blue sparks from the glossy, tumbled curls, and when he stooped down beside her, he could see the dark lashes curling on the golden tan of her skin.

Her bare back was faintly golden too, and he stretched himself quietly beside her, then pressed his mouth to the smooth back, hard enough to rouse her.

Nova gave a little startled cry, then spun over to face him; her eyes, wide now, meeting his as he leaned above her, holding her trapped within his arms, braced on either side of her body.

'Wake up, sleepy head. What a lassie you are for dozing off like a kitten!'

'I've had such a hectic time lately!' she told him, adding wickedly, 'So hectic, in fact, that I've toyed with the idea of yelling for help several times!'

The light in his eyes deepened, and a slow, threatening smile curved his lips. 'I don't recommend that ye should try it,' he warned.

'Pooh! Who's afraid of you?' Nova laughed, reaching up to ruffle the dark red hair. He pulled the small hand down and kissed the soft palm.

'You are!' he stated calmly and matter of factly and grinned as she closed her eyes quickly against the knowledge in his.

'Seriously, sweetheart! I'm starving—let's have tea. Then, remembering that we have a long day ahead tomorrow, starting out early to spend a few hours with Lossie at Strontian, I suggest we get back and have an early night.'

'Certainly, my lord! If you will just remove your considerable bulk . . .' Nova pushed hard against his muscular, bare brown chest, ineffectually until he laughingly sprang up, swinging her with him easily.

'My lassie,' he said, white teeth gleaming, 'I canna tell ye how much I'm looking forward to carrying ye into my stronghold.' He held her in his arms, closely, his eyes on the upturned face, blushing rosily.

'Oh, darling! It couldn't be better than the time we've had here,' she whispered.

'Can it not? We'll see . . .' and he bent his head with sudden passion to the soft rosy mouth of his wife. He raised his head after a long moment. 'Tea can wait a while longer,' he stated hoarsely.

For a brief moment of rebellion against his overwhelming masculinity Nova murmured a protest, 'Oh, Ross! No—please, not h—' Then the sensation of falling, to stop gently against the springy turf in the privacy of the sheltered hollow, took away her breath. The trees and the sky were suddenly blotted out by his broad shoulders, and she closed her eyes helplessly as his lips found hers again.

'Perhaps he is right, it will be even more wonderful at Glencurran, but—,' obstinately, 'I'm sure it couldn't be! I'll be content if it's as much! I really *must* learn to manage him a little though, he is so domin . . .'

It was her last coherent thought for some time . . .